The Rose on the Ash-Heap

Published by Barfield Press

Other books by Owen Barfield:

Eager Spring
Night Operation
This Ever Diverse Pair
The Case for Anthroposophy
Poetic Diction

Forthcoming new editions:

The Silver Trumpet
Orpheus: A Poetic Drama
English People
Short stories
Poetry

www.owenbarfield.org

Owen Barfield

The Rose on the Ash-Heap

Barfield Press

Series Editor: Dr. Jane Hipolito

Published by Barfield Press UK
Oxford, England

This First Edition, 2009

A catalogue record for this book is available from the British Library.

The Rose on the Ash-Heap by Owen Barfield
ISBN 978-0-9559582-2-9

Printed on paper with Sustainable Forestry Initiative (SFI) accreditation.

INTRODUCTION

The Rose on the Ash-Heap is a myth for our time, a complex and deeply imaginative exploration of three intertwining themes: love, imagination, and the evolution of modern consciousness. At once fairy tale, culture criticism, intimate romance and apocalyptic vision, it centers on the power of love and imagination to awaken, focus, mobilize, and ennoble the human spirit even in the bleakest circumstances. As Owen Barfield brilliantly demonstrates, love and imagination are truly significant capacities; indeed, the fate of the world may depend upon our exercising them.

The genre which he chose for *The Rose on the Ash-Heap* is the *märchen*, a fairy tale with magical and supernatural elements. Like the German Romantic authors, for whom the *märchen* was a favorite form, Barfield had a deep respect for the truthfulness of the imagination, and used fantasy as a means of penetrating the mysteries of the human condition. He also shared the German Romantics' attentiveness to the Eternal-Feminine. Indeed, *The Rose on the Ash-Heap* can be seen as an extended meditation on the concluding lines of Goethe's poetic drama *Faust*:

> The Eternal-Feminine
> Draws us onward.

In his commentary on these lines, Charles Passage notes that "The Eternal-Feminine is the unfailing inspiration, the moving force giving impetus in earthly life as in the life hereafter to strive from lesser stages upward toward infinite perfection. That perfection is Love; in Dante's final line of the *Paradiso*, 'the love that moves the sun and the other stars'."[1] Each of the seven sections of *The Rose on the Ash-Heap* reveals a distinct, significant aspect of how this "moving force" participates in the on-going evolution of love and imagination within human consciousness. In the first section, we meet the Eternal-Feminine as the Romantic impulse, working transformatively within the individual psyche like the beautiful, wise temple dancer who inspires the young Sultan's ardor; in the dances she teaches on her westward journey through Asia and Europe, Barfield traces the lovely "choreography" of the Romance tradition. The second section of the *märchen* specifically connects the Eternal-Feminine with the Romantic Movement in England. Here, the beautiful dancer is known by Wordsworth's name for her, Lucy; she is the adoptive daughter of the Lord of Albion, and with him guides and guards all that is good in the English spirit.

Bit by bit, however, Barfield shows, the graceful, coherent wisdom of temple, palace, and the old Romances has been supplanted by modern consciousness. In "Autem", an as yet unpublished essay which he wrote toward the end of 1928, during the same period when he was composing *The Rose on the Ash-Heap*, Barfield describes the modern situation as follows:

---

[1] See *Faust, Part One and Part Two*, by Johann Wolfgang von Goethe. Translated, with an introduction and notes, by Charles E. Passage (New York and London: Macmillan Publishing Co., 1965), page 413.

We discover that we can only "contemplate" another thing or being by ceasing to be it and conversely that we can never "contemplate" what in the deepest sense we are (i.e. we can never "know ourselves"). This sounds unimpeachable. And as *tendency* it is true. In actual fact there is a force which is overcoming this tendency at every moment. All human intercourse depends on the functioning in some slight degree of this force; for without it another soul would either be so detached from me as to be undistinguishable from a lifeless object, or it would disappear into me altogether. This force is known as love. Its whole nature is that it enables me to become another soul *and yet* to remain separate, to go out into another being and yet remain within myself. Its whole function is to mediate between the One and the Many.[2]

This situation is vividly dramatized in sections III through VII of *The Rose on the Ash-Heap*.

Section III introduces us to the Eternal-Feminine as the *Tertium Quid*, the essential "third thing" which bridges the gap between self and other in modern consciousness, and enables true self-knowledge.[3] Barfield's loving, insightful

---

[2] Quoted in *Owen Barfield: Romanticism Come of Age: A Biography*, by Simon Blaxland-de Lange (Forest Row, England: Temple Lodge Publishing, 2006), pages 166-167. Barfield wrote "Autem" as part of his extended vigorous debate with C. S. Lewis concerning the relation of imagination to truth. For further information about this debate, see Lionel Adey's book, *C. S. Lewis's "Great War" with Owen Barfield*.

[3] One indication of the importance of the "third thing" for Barfield is that *Tertium Quid* was the working title of his *märchen*.

THE ROSE ON THE ASH-HEAP

portrayal makes clear that even the finest poets and philosophers of our time tend to lack this "third thing", the capacity to meet others' real-life needs empathetically. And thus, although Sultan learns much from his new friends, the Poet and Philosopher, he recognizes that they cannot assuage his intense grieving for his Lady. He travels to Earth's westernmost point, where, alone under the night sky, he has a life-changing epiphany: love and imagination are spiritual powers, and their "unfailing inspiration" unites human hearts with each other and with the celestial spheres. This crucial turning-point in Sultan's experience occurs in the central section of *The Rose on the Ash-Heap*. It is the pivotal event in the entire *märchen*, for here we, with Sultan, learn what the Eternal-Feminine calls each of us to do in the present world. We must use imagination as a depth-perception lens on modern civilization, and our love must mature from *eros* into *agape*.

Sections V and VI of *The Rose on the Ash-Heap* present the modern world-view as a vividly imagined dystopia — Abdolbion, a vast, multi-continental realm whose cultural capital is an amusement park atop an ash-heap. In this utterly materialistic, ruthlessly wasteful modern mindscape, demeaning stereotypes of race and gender prevail; love is confidently assumed to be sexual satisfaction, nothing more; and imagination is the pliant prisoner of marketing. Abdol, the founder and perpetual governor of Abdolbion, is a petrochemicals entrepreneur and expert designer of commercial media. Like Dostoevsky's Grand Inquisitor, he cynically caters to his subjects' lowest appetites, providing creature comforts, sensory thrills, and total freedom from personal responsibility. Abdolbion's residents are mere consumers, mindlessly absorbed in the instant gratification of their infotainment environment and forgetful of their cultural heritage.

In Barfield's analysis, this is not at all an acceptable situation, for the Abdolbionic ethos is not passive or neutral. Rather, it is the counter-force of the Eternal-Feminine, and it is dangerously aggressive; left unchecked, it will devastate the ecosphere and gobble up the human spirit. It can only be defeated by the deep-rooted Sun-wisdom of the Rose, the Eternal-Feminine, living in the selfless, courageous deeds of free human beings. The concluding section of the *märchen* discloses how the Rose's wisdom now works beneath the surface, in the space foresightedly prepared by Albion's Lord; there, love and imagination create balance and mobility in the individual psyche and engender true community.

Barfield wrote *The Rose on the Ash-Heap* in the late 1920s, a time of widespread societal and economic instability. Throughout the decade, he worked wholeheartedly for constructive change, participating actively in the Social Credit Union and the Anthroposophical Society and writing for a variety of progressive English periodicals. Simultaneously, he pursued the intensive study of language, literature, the "Rose" tradition, the nature of imagination, and the psychology of love which resulted in his first three books — *The Silver Trumpet* (1925), *History in English Words* (1926), and his B.Litt. thesis, *Poetic Diction* (completed in 1926-1927 but not published until 1928).

The Rose on the Ash-Heap imaginatively epitomizes Barfield's spiritual development during those years. And as Thomas Kranidas has perceptively noted, it also provides "a kind of epitome in fantasy of the basic issues" of *English People*, Barfield's ambitious unpublished novel of English life between the First and Second World Wars, for which the *märchen* serves as epilogue. These are the basic issues for us in the twenty-first century, as well: "the dire confrontation of spiritual and materialistic forces, the apparent defeat of spirit in our time and its ultimate triumph."[4]

Jane Hipolito

---

[4] *A Barfield Sampler: Poetry and Fiction by Owen Barfield*, edited by Jeanne Clayton Hunter and Thomas Kranidas (Albany, NY: State University of New York Press, 1993), pages 94-95.

FOREWORD
BY OWEN BARFIELD

IT IS NOW accepted on nearly all sides that the seeds of destruction were inherent in Western civilization before the War began. It may be that peace will be restored and immediate physical destruction averted. But if so, although some poisonous growths will no doubt have been lopped, the same seeds will still be present with their germinating power unchecked. A terrific shock will have stirred us to the depths and made us watchful, but we dare not assume that it will have made us wise.

If the great heritage of the West is to be preserved, we shall want a new insight, not only to recognize the rotten patches for what they are, instead of welcoming them as triumphs of progress, but also to enable us to penetrate to the core of Western Civilization and draw up its health and goodness to the surface. In the world of the spirit there are shapely things of which our monstrosities are perversions, witnessing to their existence and demonstrating their strength.

The Rose on the Ash-Heap is a "Märchen", 26,600 words in length. Sultan, the central figure, travels daily further from the East and is eventually lost in a country not unlike the advertisement-machine and sex-ridden Eur-America which we were getting to know before the War. Formerly ruled and guided by the Lord of Albion, it is now under the total dominion of Abdol, who needs no secret police to enforce his highly centralised authority, since he uses the technique not of scarcity but of plenty — *panem et circenses* in a literal sense.

XVI THE ROSE ON THE ASH-HEAP

The story tells of Sultan's many and varied experiences, his encounters, his efforts and his lapses, until at last he finds his way out, not (like some mystics of today) by retracing his steps to the East whence he started forth, but rather by pursuing his westward journey to its utmost limit. There he finds a special master key. This he takes back with him on his final return to the West, where Abdol's blatant and horrible Fun Fair is in progress. It lets him in to the secret Circus under the great ash-heap in its midst. After long and arduous training he himself becomes a circus-rider, is united to the daughter of the Lord of Albion — the bride whom he has so long been seeking — and together with her participates in the apocalyptic end of the Fair and of Abdol's reign.

1993

I

THE MIDNIGHT AIR was thunderous and oppressive.

In the inky darkness of the seraglio nothing moved; nothing broke the mysterious brooding warmth; everywhere stillness reigned, sleep and light breathing and the memory of love. All night the young Sultan had been giving himself body and soul, in mystic sacrificial delight of self-abandonment; and he arose now from the arms of the youngest and fairest of his wives and paced uneasily out of the women's apartments into the courtyard. There were no stars, but it mattered nothing. Here he could breathe more freely, here he could dull the aching of his sick heart with the opiate of reflection. The Sultan began to walk round his courtyard, his hands clasped behind his back and his eyes bent on the ground. Very soon however, when that simple rhythmic motion lost its power to soothe, he turned, and crossed the courtyard diagonally. But when he reached the centre, overcome at the same moment with the weariness that accompanies sorrow and the weariness that follows abundance of love, the Lord of all the Asias and hereditary High Priest of all their religions sank on his knees, rested his arms on the low wall that ran round the tinkling fountain and laid his head upon them.

The Sultan prayed. First he offered up his spirit to all the gods with the same mystic intensity of self-abandonment that he had practised within the seraglio. But soon he began to pray more personally, and even more intensely. And above all he prayed to Shiva, the dancing god, the Shining One. He prayed that Shiva would help

him, either to win for his thousandth wife or else for ever
to forget the beautiful white-skinned dancer in the Temple,
who had destroyed his peace of mind. He prayed so long
that at last as he knelt there in his weariness, prayer passed
over into sleep and sleep in its turn into dream. And then
the Sultan dreamed that his prayer was answered. It
seemed that Shiva brought him the white-skinned darling.
"For," said the god, with a twinkling smile, "you will
certainly never forget her"! Thus, Shiva brought the
temple-dancer to the palace and they two, the dancer and
the Sultan, were betrothed and at last united. And then
there followed, in his dream, a strange and a wonderfully
sweet time. It seemed to him that he introduced many
changes into the customs of the palace. The first thing he
did was to expel utterly from the court in one wailing dusky
procession all his other wives and concubines. Soon after
he had done that, he broke down much of the heavy
lattice-work with which the windows of the women's
apartments were darkened. Next he cut down the
luxuriant overgrowth of olive and fig, so that daylight
poured, for the first time since it had been built, into nearly
every corner of the seraglio. And each time, so it seemed
to him, it was his love for the white-skinned dancer that
impelled him to make the change, his love and her bold
example. For already, even before they were united, she
had withdrawn the veil from her glorious little face and
had announced as she did so, with a low and joyous laugh,
her determination never never to wear it again. And, after
that, the uninterrupted vision of the two red lips which had
laughed as she spoke — a sight to which the young Sultan

was so totally unaccustomed — had seemed to enter his very blood, making it dance in his veins and giving him courage for every further innovation which she suggested.

Days, weeks, months passed by in the dream and still the two had no other thought but to wander through the empty sunlit seraglio hand in hand, playing, bathing, laughing, caressing, sleeping together when they were exhausted, until the Sultan's senses became verily confused. There were strange moments when he could scarcely tell which it was that he beheld, the full, rich, life-giving streams of light that poured down upon him from the Eastern sun or that other mystical glow which her blood sent glowing through her warm flesh into his eyes, as they lay together in the shade of the trees by the cool fountain and he gazed and gazed at the mystery of her body, until she leaned fragrantly forward and blinded him once more in a bewildering cloud of sweet touches. And afterwards his memory would confuse the delicious coolness of the breeze that rustled through the leaves of the fig-trees and played about his forehead and eyes and limbs with that other marvellously sweet coolness of her arms around his head or of her light and lake-washed thigh resting like a butterfly's wing upon his own. Is it, he would ask himself, the sunset that diffuses this calm radiance over the green turf and the dark green leaves? Is it not rather the golden halo, made eternal, of her hair about her face as it hung above mine suspended in an ecstasy of passionate hesitation between the last kiss and the next?

At last, one day, in his dream, the Sultan was walking in the garden alone, pondering as always on the new life of endless rapture with his beloved. He heard a light step behind him and with a secret smile stopped, without looking round, as if arrested by his own thoughts. He knew that she would come up nearer, that she would think he was unaware of her presence, that she would surprise him with a delicious caress. He waited until he could feel the warmth of her breast, as it all but touched his back, and then the warmth of her two arms, as they crept stealthily round his sides, seeking to encircle him wholly before they touched him. And then he closed his eyes and in the extremity of bliss could not repress one long-drawn trembling sigh, which, by shifting his position slightly on the stones, awakened him from his dream. He found himself lying cramped and huddled by the fountain in the midst of his own courtyard, the morning sun pouring pitilessly on to his back and bathing it in a sickening warmth, which was just beginning to creep round his sides and bake the whole of his body.

For a long time the Sultan refused to admit to himself that the dream was indeed over, nestling his head on to the unyielding stone of the fountain's rim and praying wildly to Shiva to let him dream again, only to let him dream again. But it was all of no avail. And at last, after looking in a rather shamefaced way round the courtyard, to see if any of his servants were yet stirring, he hurried indoors to his own rooms, where he summoned two slaves, who bathed and anointed him and then dressed him as well as they could for his impatient and restless movements. At last, however, he was free of their attentions. Taking no one with him, he ran through the empty streets to the

Temple and knocked on the door. He did not doubt of finding someone awake, for he knew that in the Temple there must be someone always awake.

It was the Priest himself, an old man in flowing white robes, whom the Sultan's knock had called back to earth from some unfathomable depths of meditation, who opened the door to him. The young Sultan explained his errand and, as he proceeded, his greedy words seemed to kindle a smouldering fire in the deep eyes of the old man.

"Madman!" he exclaimed, drawing himself up to his full height and staring fiercely and fearlessly at the royal visitor. "Sacrilegious monster! Are you not aware that she has already taken her vows?"

"I care nothing for her vows or any vows, Father. I only know that I cannot forego my desire, I only know that my desire is so beautiful and so strong that the Eternal himself would not have me forego it. Where is she?"

"She is within," replied the tall and bearded serenity in a grave voice; and he pointed to a thick black curtain which hid the entrance to another apartment giving on the Temple.

"Then out of my way, Old Man!" shouted the Sultan suddenly, with an ugly threatening gesture. But the Priest did not move, and, in spite of himself, the impatient young monarch was afraid to jostle him. They looked at one another.

"Father," said the Sultan at last, in a small, broken voice, "I would enter the Temple-service, would become a devotee and learn to dance your intense dances to the glory of God. I know not what words fell from my mouth a moment back. Think that I was possessed by the Evil One!" The priest gave him a swift searching look.

"You have other duties, Sultan!" he said sternly.

At last, however, the young Sultan succeeded in persuading the old man that he was in earnest. He declared that his brother would make an abler ruler than himself and one no less willing to be guided by the wisdom of the Temple. He said, and with truth, that he himself had long heard the call to the sacred life, had heard it no less clearly than he had heard the call of his blood. Sinking his head, he admitted to the reverend Father than his youth and inexperience were as yet ill able to distinguish the one voice wholly from the other. At last, the old Priest consented to his request and bade him return to the Temple on the morrow.

All that day and the following night were passed by the feverish Sultan alone in his own apartments. When at last he returned to the Temple in the morning, he was astonished to find the door open and everywhere an appearance of great disorder. With a sinking heart he hastened into the empty building and passed with echoing steps up to the altar, where he found the holy Father kneeling alone with bowed head and streaming eyes. He seemed like a figure carved in stone. At last he rose and turned and faced the young Sultan.

"Father!" he cried out in a loud voice, dismayed by the lineaments of a sorrow infinitely deeper than his own, "Father, what terrible disaster has stricken you since I was here yesterday?"

"She has fled," replied the Priest.

"Whither — Why?" cried the miserable Sultan.

"The dreams of a monarch," replied the old man, eyeing the young one sternly and significantly, "are more powerful than the dreams of a dog." The Sultan knelt down at the reverend Father's feet and wept bitterly.

"Father!" he said. "I am but a boy of no understanding at all. Absolve me from the professions I made to you here yesterday. Make me free to seek her."

"You are free," said the old Priest solemnly and he raised his hand in blessing. "Many devotees will be born and will serve in this Temple and will die. We shall not need your services my son!" And he continued, out of all the bitterness in his heart: "No, we shall not need any more the services of living men, but only now of spinning tops. The Eternal has taken her from us. The Eternal be praised! My son, my son, I will conceal it from you no longer, for there is no longer any reason to conceal it. Know then, that I myself had long been *hoping* for the day when you might come to me, as you came yesterday, and with that demand. For while she was here, we had use for *men*, for men who must indeed, until the time of purification, hear the call of the Eternal in the call of the blood. In truth it was for that very reason that she was here. But now the Eternal has taken her from us! The Eternal be praised! For the true votaries are few and they grow daily fewer. Spinning-tops enough have we here and more than enough; for spinning-tops do not make" (the Priest laid his hands with a mournful smile on the young Sultan's head) "the mistake which you made! God has taken her from us! God be praised! God forbid I should

persuade *you*, my son, to stay here and become — a
spinning-top. For the way of the spinning-top is the way
of wood, but your way shall be the way of blood. Go then,
seek her — and with my blessing!" The Sultan, who was
bewildered by the Father's words, and at the same time
deeply and mysteriously moved, at last took courage to ask
him which way the Holy One, the white-skinned dancer,
had gone.

"Westward!" replied the Priest.

After having abdicated and made the necessary
arrangements that his brother might rule over Asia in his
stead, the young Sultan took a long farewell of his mother
and father and set out on his journey. He soon learned that
the fair dancer had passed swiftly on before him, rarely
staying long in one place. And if it was easy to follow her
movements (since, wherever she passed, her memory
lingered), yet it proved to be impossible, try as he would, to
intercept or overtake her. For so secret were those
movements that it was only after she had left each place that
the people there began to realise even that such a person
had been among them. At last, therefore, taught by many
bitter disappointments, the Sultan abandoned all his clever
attempts to foretell her route and anticipate her and
contented himself with following as close behind as rumour
made possible, always hoping against hope that somewhere
someday she would protract her stay just long enough for
him to come up with her, and throw himself at her feet.

It appeared that she was earning a livelihood, as she
travelled, by teaching music and dances to the good people

through whose country she passed. And these dances proved to be the Sultan's best means of tracking her, for, after she had left, they usually became fashionable with all classes, and that so quickly that he was enabled on one or two occasions to come within a few miles of her person. To each people she taught a different kind of step and movement with different music suited to their natures. The Sultan, who was himself quick and impressionable, was astonished at the variety of her invention and the tact with which she suited her gifts in each case to the receiver. In truth, the long prayers and fasting vigils which she had formerly kept in the Temple must have already taught her to read deep into the hearts of men, so that, now that the time had come for her to use such powers, she was not found wanting.

In Western Asia, through which he passed at the outset of his journey, the Sultan found, left behind by the White-skinned One, swaying measures and langorous tunes, tunes which came to him like a perfumed breath from the seraglio, and brought tears to his eyes and almost persuaded him to turn back home and seek out his youngest wives and, above all, a certain little concubine, whom he had heartlessly abandoned. Indeed, he was able to restrain himself from this course only by the reflection that, so far, wherever he had come, he had found no lack of such feminine consolation. Not long after this, his search led him on into Southern Europe, where the melancholy soldiers of Hellas welcomed him kindly to their camp-fires and taught him (a very different matter) the military measures, in which she had instructed *them*, as she passed. Hurrying on through Ausonia, where he could find few traces of her, since the folk were already so firmly wedded to certain wild dances of their own, that they had refused to listen, he then followed her footsteps into the high country north of the Pillars of Hercules. Here he was overjoyed to find the memory of the Holy One still warm in the hearts of prince and peasant alike, and, as usual, he sought to invoke her gentle spirit into his presence by acquainting himself with the measures and music which she had left behind her. By great good fortune he found lodging with a wealthy nobleman, who had been summoned that very night to afford hospitality to his sovereign on the occasion of a royal progress. The most sumptuous entertainments had been provided to amuse the royal visitant and in the course of the evening the courtiers and ladies-in-waiting performed by moonlight one of the 'new dances.' The ravished Sultan thought he had never seen anything more tender and more beautiful, as the men and women, dressed in rich and brilliant brocades, circled slowly and gracefully round one another, gliding over the turf like gorgeous swans. Endless the circlings of each couple appeared, endless as the untiring movements of the planets in their orbits, and as they danced, each courtier sang to the lady with whom he was dancing, and at whom he was gazing.

At first he sang,

> *Sweet, who dost hold my heart*
> *Fast immurèd in those eyes,*
> *Approach, oh, ease my smart,*
> *Ere thy piteous caitiff dies!*

And then, as the dance moved towards an end and the music died gently away in a plucking of muted strings, each dancer came gravely up beside his mistress and, the two of them singing, as he did so, in the sweetest possible harmony the last two lines of the song,

What is eternal? This:
Thou givest me a kiss.

he allowed his lips to rest on hers so softly that you were scarcely aware when the singing had ceased and the kissing begun.

As for the lonely and travel-tired Sultan, it seemed to him at that moment that the Holy One from the Temple was indeed beside him and that he had known what it was to rest in her arms. And yet this passing dream of bliss was the prelude to a new dismay. For the next morning, he discovered a serious difference of opinion among his hosts concerning the direction in which the dancer had departed. It was the first time this had happened. To some, apparently, she had announced her intention of returning to Asia, while others swore that they had learnt from her own lips that she meant to travel farther westward, even as far west as the land of Albion. The distracted Sultan, not knowing whom to believe, decided, after much hesitation, to continue westward. "I will never return to Asia, unless I must," he thought, "for fear of being dragged back into the ancient ways."

He crossed the sea, therefore, to Albion, and, as soon as he had stepped ashore, fell on his face and gave thanks to the Eternal for bringing him safe over the water. For hitherto all his journey had been on land, and the black threatening waves had terrified him.

The Sultan rose from the ground. There seemed to be something purifying in the very air of this new country. Strange new impulses stirred in him. Full of the memory of the beautiful dance which he had witnessed, he suddenly knelt again and vowed passionately to Shiva that he would never again lie in a woman's arms, until he had found his own.

Alas, the Sultan was confronted with greater difficulties in Albion than he had yet experienced in the whole of his travels. It was not only that he was obliged, owing to his unpopularity with the people, to conceal his oriental origin under the homely title of "Mr. Sultan" but he soon discovered a hopeless state of mental confusion among them, whenever he enquired for the Beloved.

The dance, which he had witnessed in his last resting-place, and which had worked so powerfully in his memory, had itself — it appeared — travelled by now into Albion, and this led many people to assert that the White-skinned One herself had passed and had been seen by them. On questioning these people more closely, however, he always found that they were mistaken. On the other hand, there was a mysterious tradition of a divinely fair woman, a virgin goddess, who, under the name of "Lady" or, as some said, "Lucy", dwelt secretly in the heart of the country. Unfortunately the Sultan could make nothing certain of all this. Sometimes he fancied that the Holy One herself was indeed already in the heart of Albion, possibly quite near to him, having been obliged, as he himself had been, to disguise her identity under a more native-sounding name. And then he even began to call her "Lady" in his dreams. Sometimes, however, he doubted if she had ever come to Albion at all. And at last, hearing a rumour from the North-East that she had indeed returned to Asia long ago, he himself suddenly faced about and set out for home.

The journey back was long and wearisome, but at last it was accomplished. From the smart young dervishes who were lounging about the Temple precincts he learned that the Holy One had indeed returned during his absence, and had visited the Temple, where she had spent three unbroken days and nights in meditation. The young priests smirked a little, as they told him this, evidently regarding such devotion as a mark of rusticity, and he could see from their eyes how glad they were that she had gone away again and that the old Priest, unable to support the shock of her second departure for the West, had sunk beneath the weight of years and sorrow into the grave. She had been there, then! And while he was in Albion! The Sultan, as he heard the news, felt at first ready to follow the old Priest, in his bitterness and despair. But instead of doing so, he found out the whereabouts of the little concubine and broke his vow. And after he had done so, his despair was greater than ever.

The Sultan stayed long enough at home to learn that his brother was still ruling in the ancient ways, carried forward rather by habit than by any new inspiration from the Temple, and that his mother and father were both dead. And then, overcome with loneliness, older, and without even the hope which had buoyed him up on his first departure, or the confidence which an unbroken vow might have assured him, he set forth a second time in the wake of the Beloved. This time rumour led him into Northern Europe. He found himself among a fair-haired people, whose fresh and frank-looking faces — especially while they were still young — touched even his sad heart to a passing gaiety. And he came one evening to a delightful clean little town, on the banks of the Ister. Here he put up in an ancient inn with pleasantly carved and pointed gables, and after taking supper, he walked out into the street. The folk were making holiday, strolling to and fro in couples and dancing in the open spaces, and the long plaits of the maidens flew out gaily behind them in the summer breeze. And, behold, something, some quality in the dance which they were dancing, told the Sultan that he had not been mistaken. Lady herself must have been here a short while since. Following his usual custom, therefore, he procured himself a few nights later an invitation to a fashionable ball. He arrived before the dancing began. No sooner did the musicians strike up than the most indescribable sensations filled his breast. For, as he became accustomed to the undulating rhythm, which was totally new to him and heard the strange voluptuous melody which was woven on it, on the one hand the langours of the seraglio began to steal over his senses and to sap away all the vigour of his spirit, and on the other hand this very rhythm and melody spoke to him, more loudly and more clearly than any music had done before, of his own, of the Beloved, of Lady herself, stirring up in hitherto unfathomed depths of his soul the most unspeakable hopes of future bliss. Hardly knowing where he was, and still dreaming furiously of the paradise of her arms, the Sultan found himself led up to a partner, a beautiful blonde, before whom he stood stupid and abashed, as he endeavoured to collect his wits. He began by explaining to her humbly his ignorance of the step and of the measure, but she promised to teach him everything, and to his amazement, instead of first instructing him to bow and kneel, and to go through all the previous motions which Western decorum prescribed, she proceeded at once to draw him arm gently round her slim little waist.

"I see you will make a quick scholar!" she exclaimed with an understanding laugh, as she perceived how gladly he allowed the arm to remain where she had placed it, and in a moment they were gliding like a single creature over the polished floor. For a long time, endlessly revolving together, they danced in the gravest silence. But at last the pretty blonde looked up into the Sultan's face and asked him, "Well, and how do you like it, Herr Sultan?"

"I feel," he replied, "as if it must go on for ever!" For he was still dreaming that he held Lady herself in his arms. The blonde tossed her head and laughed up into his eyes.

"Clever scholar!" she said, archly. "So you have found out already! How did you know? That is *exactly* what you ought to feel!"

Long after that evening, as he wandered wearily on, still pursuing the faint echoes of Lady's lovely melodies among the hearts of Bohemian peasants and Flemish mercers, Sultan often recalled to himself the words of the laughing little blonde by the banks of the Ister, and then he wondered what mysteries might have passed between the Eternal and the White-skinned One during her last long vigil in the Temple. What had the Eternal taught her to teach? And to what end?

II

THE LORD OF Albion was pacing up and down the great hall of the palace beside the Princess, his newly adopted daughter. Suddenly he turned and summoned an equerry.

"Sire?"

"Our time is short. Are the subterranean works completed?"

"They are completed, Sire."

"To the last prop?"

"To the last prop."

"The Marquee?" The Equerry reassured him.

"And the Stables?"

"Sire, every one of your orders has been carried out in the minutest detail!"

"That is well!" said the monarch. "Very well! At all costs we must preserve the breed!" He paused and reflected for a moment.

"I thank you, Equerry!" he added, "you may go!" And his voice softened, as he repeated more significantly, "You understand what I mean — you may go now, all of you!" But the Equerry fell on his knees.

"Oh my Lord," he cried, "still keep me by your side! Let me continue to serve you in whatever station you shall dictate. Only do not turn me wholly away. Do not force me into the slave-mills of Abdol. I am not fitted for them — and outside the Palace to-day there is no other livelihood possible."

The Lord of Albion was deeply moved. He laid his hands on the Equerry's head.

"Courage!" he said, "you will find your way back to us at last, if you really desire it! Now go!"

He turned to the Princess.

"Lucy, my dear!" he said, "it is to-night! We have nothing to fear — only we must be ready." She bowed to him and retired to her own apartments.

No sooner had she reached them, than a Lady-in-Waiting entered and informed her that a stranger, an oriental gentleman, who refused to give his name, greatly desired an audience. The Princess commanded that he should be admitted and in a very few minutes a footman ushered the stranger in and closed the door.

"Lady!"

"Sultan!"

"Lady — I have found you at last!"

"Ah!"

"And for ever!" She did not answer.

He knelt before her feet.

"Lady! Lady! I was so lonely!"

"Yet you have known many women!"

"Then most of all, Lady, then most of all! Loneliest of all when, the tapers extinguished and the curtains drawn, I lost all sight of the Eternal's glorious sunlight, lost all sight of the vast concourse of my suffering fellow-creatures and wilfully beheld instead nothing but one pitiful and painted phantom of my own desire, which, even so, I struggled in vain to possess."

The Princess of Albion did not reply.

"You — you forgive?" asked Sultan at last in a low and tremulous voice.

"Freely!"

"And your father — I may see him?"

"Not to-day!"

"Will he, too, forgive?"

"Yes, but he cannot forget." She raised him gently from his knees and, taking him in her arms, kissed him once on the lips.

"Go now, Sultan dear!" she commanded, "and — and return!"

"Lady, Lady, you will be here again tomorrow, in the same place, at the same time?"

She nodded, and turned away her head to hide the blinding tears.

It was late that night before Sultan slept, for he sat up, talking with his host, being anxious to learn all he could about the Lord of Albion, his history, and his ways.

"Our beloved Lord of Albion," explained the innkeeper, "is the Emperor of many western lands. He has long been seeking, after his own fashion, to extend his dominion, which is no dominion, but perfect freedom, over the whole earth, but at present he is sore bestead and I know not how long his kingdom, even so wide as it is, will stand. The common people, it is true, love him and trust him, but they no longer trust the nobility. This must in any case be an evil thing, but it might not have been dangerous to the sovereign's personal life and liberty, did there not stand unseen behind the indistinguishable mass of the commonalty, pouring his subtle poison at every crevice into the weakness of their imaginations and the strength of their passions, an inconceivably wealthy and powerful private citizen, named Abdol. You must know that this Abdol has long been jealous of the Lord of Albion, and at last, through his great deftness with money and his skill in commerce, has insinuated his will into the finest vessels of Albion's body politic so that, in the opinion of many, *he* is now the true Lord of Albion — or "Abdolbion", as our wits call it. Even the palace is heavily mortgaged to him, or at any rate the gardens, for some say that the building itself is still free of all incumbrances. And, Sir, the result of all this is that our dominion is indeed being extended over the earth, but in a very different manner from that which our Lord had imagined. It is in fact a dominion of Abdolbion. "Work for me!" says Abdol to all the world, "and then buy what I wish to sell you, or I shall starve you and the captains of the Lord of Albion will poison you with gas out of my tubes!"

"But do not any of the captains — the nobility — support the sovereign?" asked Sultan.

"Many of them would, were they not too stupid to understand, or too completely in Abdol's power to be able to move," replied Mine Host.

"What then can be the origin of this terrible jealousy?"

"That is a long story," said the innkeeper. "You must know that it has long been the first desire of our Sovereign to maintain in this country an excellent breed of horses. He believes that it is the special task of Albion to preserve this legacy from the days when chivalry was a power in Europe in order that, when the time comes, she may be able to distribute it all over the world. Now this particular duty he handed over on his accession almost entirely to the nobility, who, however, soon began to neglect it. Pretending to themselves that they were 'preserving the breed', they gave in fact all their time and attention to trivialities such as hunting, racing and betting.

Their talk was indeed all of horses, but they had forgotten how to groom them and, what is worse, they had forgotten how to *look at* them! Meanwhile the tenants on their estates and indeed the common people in general were also forgotten, left to fester in their hovels, or kept quiet, when necessary, with a whiff of grapeshot.

"Then," said Sultan, "those hard-faced, beady-eyed, stupid-looking people whom I saw riding about the grounds of the palace in hats that appeared to me like the skulls of bald negroes,[1] were no doubt the nobility?"

"They were," replied the innkeeper. "Now it happens that Abdol was *also* interested in horses. He reared them in large numbers in the arid deserts of Arabia, the land of his birth, and then sought to dispose of them in Albion at high prices. We all admit, Sir, that Abdol's horses have many good qualities, but they have many serious defects. They are swift, Sir, amazingly swift, but they are often malicious and apt to throw even the experienced rider. Now the Lord of Albion perceived this defect clearly. One day, therefore, calling the nobility together, he explained to them the difference between Abdol's equine breed and his own, exhorting them in the most earnest tones to keep the two strains distinct and to do all that they could to keep Abdol's stallions out of the country. The nobles appeared

---

[1] See the footnote on page 63.

to listen respectfully enough, but alas, they were already too besotted by their everlasting racing and hunting to be able even to *distinguish* Abdol's breed from the native one. Consequently — owing to Abdol's aptitude for commerce, which I have already mentioned — his stock increased by leaps and bounds, and even at last began to oust the true breed of Albion altogether from the country. At last, unsupported in this all-important matter by his worthless nobles, the Lord of Albion, in order to demonstrate as signally as possible his opinion of the danger and his contempt for the ultimate uselessness of Abdol's breed, made a significant public gesture.

Abdol had organised an enormous race-meeting, at which, so cunningly did he advertise it, he knew that the cream of fashion would attend, in order to watch the races and publish the flimsy and expensive garments of their wives. Everything went as Abdol had intended. The meeting was even patronised by the Lord of Albion himself. Crowds attended, and Abdol's own great black pedigree horses came home first in nearly every race, amid loud cheers from grandstand and cheap enclosure alike. Only in the last race of all did anything unforeseen occur. For – listen, Sir! – the Lord of Albion, who had entered a beast of his own for this number, actually came up to the starting-line at the last moment, himself — *riding on a donkey!* Imagine it! He dismissed his jockey and, starting off with the rest, came in *last* by hundreds of yards — but amid deafening cheers from the cheap enclosure. Indeed, although the nobles hissed and turned up their noses, the people stormed through the fences on to the course, shouldered their monarch, and almost overwhelmed poor Neddy with thistles and caresses.

This characteristically eccentric action created a deep impression in the country, and shortly after it occurred, Abdol, who is nothing if not far-sighted, suddenly appeared to lose all interest in horses, though of course his strain, so deeply had it penetrated, is still the predominant one in our stables. He returned for a while to his native land and there interested himself in mineral oils, which he soon found out how to produce in infinitely large quantities. These oils are adapted for use in a variety of engines, which have already, so Abdol himself loudly and often proclaims, made horses of any kind, whether his own or ours, unnecessary. And so for the last ten years, Sir, he has been pouring these highly inflammable oils into our country at a rate far greater than our people can pay for. For at the same time, you must know, he has a firmer control than ever of our money and cannot bring himself to let us have enough of it to buy his goods. Meanwhile the wretched man, torn between his two conflicting desires, grows more jealous and revengeful every day. In the strident and hideous tones of secret despair he invokes louder and louder; and through a continually increasing ingenuity of amplifying devices, his starving slaves to spend the money which he refuses to give them. And every day the tide of his unexploded oil rises higher in our land, and this time the Lord of Albion can make no gesture to stop it. And where it will end, Sir, I believe no one can yet say."

The hour was late. The innkeeper had spoken in a manner which not only showed how deeply disturbed he himself was, but communicated this uneasiness to the listener. Elated and apprehensive at the same time, Sultan went to his room, fell asleep, and dreamed. It seemed to him that he had wooed Lady after the Western manner and that she had consented to his prayers. They were united. The wedding-day passed deliciously, a dream within a dream, until the evening came, when he was to attend with his Beloved a grand feast given by the Lord of Albion to celebrate the happy event. Hardly had they sat down to table however, when Sultan perceived, unobtrusively seated in a far corner of the room, the little concubine who had once meant so much to him in the seraglio, and for whose sake he had later broken his vow. She kept her eyes fixed demurely upon her plate and made no movement to claim acquaintance, while Lady at any rate showed that she was totally unaware of her presence. Yet one swift glance was enough to tell Sultan that the Lord of Albion knew all. Eagerly, after the feast was over and the guests departed, did he hurry to the bridal chamber. He opened the door and approached the nuptial couch. Ah, horror of horrors! For upon the bed lay a hideous beldam, whose toothless nakedness was more disgusting than anything he had ever seen. "Stay me with flagons, and comfort me with apples!" she croaked to him, as soon as he opened the door. "Too long already, Beloved, hast thou tarried!" and, as she spoke, she rolled on the bed and stretched out lovingly towards him two black and skinny sticks of arms. Sultan sprang backward in dismay, but the hag was too quick for him. Leaping from the bed she pinioned his arms to his sides and bore him down upon it, almost suffocating him with the extremity of nausea. He struggled like a maniac to withdraw his face from those appalling breasts, and at last, with the perspiration streaming down his face, awoke to find Mine Host standing in his bedroom by the open door, seeking to fan away the suffocating smoke and reeking fumes which were pouring in at the window.

"It has begun!" he cried, seeing that his guest was awake.

"What — what has begun?"

"The contest with Abdol! The ground about the Palace must have been secretly soaked with oil for months."

"The Palace!" shouted Sultan in a terrible voice, "the Palace!" and leaping from his bed he rushed wildly through the streets to the Palace-Gardens. Alas! Where six hours before the gorgeous building had stood in all its majesty and grace, there was now nothing but one enormous heap of the finest grey ashes — not a brick, not a fragment of wall remained to reveal that this blackening heap was once the home of kings.

"But the inmates — the Royal Family!" cried the miserable Sultan to one of the bystanders — "they were of course removed long before the roof fell in?"

"On the contrary," replied the man gravely, "it is impossible that anyone in the Palace can have escaped. The whole building went up in one instantaneous roar!"

"But the Lord of Albion — " cried Sultan " — the Princess!" The bystander nodded with wide-open serious eyes that left the enquirer in no doubt of the truth.

At last, creeping round to a part of the great pyre which lay deeper in the shadow of the few surviving garden-trees than the rest, Sultan sank to the ground without a murmur. No longer did he pray to Shiva nor to any other god. He only buried his face deep deep in the soft ruin, and deeper still did he grind it in, until he positively felt and tasted the feathery ashes between his teeth.

III

THE SOLITARY TRAVELLER toiled slowly up the little flat-topped limestone hill towards the sunset, against which it was so sharply outlined. Once or twice he turned in order to rest his weary limbs and survey the wide prospect that lay stretched behind him, still, clear and beautiful in the evening light. He was now in a part of the country which had been carefully preserved and secluded from the encroachments of Abdol's factories and workmen's dwellings, and, as far as the eye could reach, it beheld nothing but fair green fields with here and there a pretty thatched cottage, sheltering one of those kindly peasants, among whom he had been living and who had advised him so persistently, out of the depths of that slow but profound nature-wisdom which was their birthright, to seek out the Poet, the Poet who, they assured him, would understand the deep sorrow which was troubling his heart so much better than they could.

The forlorn traveller had not stood long looking at the prospect, before sorrowful memories came thronging back to him and the bitter tears welled up slowly once more in his eyes. He turned quickly, as the lethargy of grief threatened to overtake him, and began plodding on. By the time he reached the Poet's dwelling, on the top of the hill, the sunset had changed to twilight and the twilight in its turn was giving way to a cool, sparkling afterglow, out of which the stars began to twinkle one by one. He knocked at the carven oak door of the dignified old stone house, and soon the Poet, an elderly and graceful man beautifully dressed in a close-fitting suit of grey velvet, welcomed him in with a kindly smile. After his host had appointed him a chamber and they had supped together in silence, the two went out through the French windows on to a balcony which commanded the whole of the Eastern prospect.

"This," said the Poet, in his musical voice, "is where, provided it is warm enough, I love to sit both day and night, alone and looking Eastward."

The traveller did not reply. The afterglow had died out of the firmament and, the night being moonless, the summer stars shone gravely down upon the pair as though from no great distance. At last the Poet spoke again, indicating the heavens with a graceful sweep of his arm.

"I always think of a beautiful summer night," he said, "as my lady's dress! It is as if she were leaning down to me and almost brushing my cheek with the golden spangles that adorn it."

Sultan once more made no reply, and after a time the Poet gently enquired who had sent him. He explained.

"Ah!" said the Poet with a smile, "even the peasants understand, after their quaint fashion, that I know — better than any other — what it is to lose the Beloved." He continued to speak much, and with great beauty of gesture and intonation, on the subject of lost love and of the pangs which it arouses in feeling hearts, and as he spoke, Sultan's own heart gradually warmed towards his host, until, in pitying the sorrows of another, he half forgot his own.

After this evening, during all the time that Sultan spent in his house, the Poet spoke to him often and sweetly on this subject. But he did more than this to aid his visitor. For, when a few days had passed, he began to discourse more freely and openly of certain mysterious consolations which the bereaved lover has a right to expect. He explained, for example, to Sultan how, had he himself not lost his Beloved, he could certainly never have been such a great Poet and, in illustration of these words, took down a lyre and sang to him many of his own poems which were piercingly beautiful and often gay even in their sadness. He told Sultan how, when the face of Nature looked plain and old and uninspiring, he could always induce the required poetic frenzy by telling himself that it was the face of his Beloved, by seeing in the blowing poppies her soft red lips, in the rounded cornfields her glowing breast, by feeling in the sunshine her kindness, and in the breeze over the meadows the sweet breath of her kisses. The Poet's manner, as he told Sultan all this, exhorting him at the same time to seek out similar consolations for himself, grew more and more genial and animated. And he went on to explain how, for his part, he found it enabled him, not merely to compose the most delightful and piercing-sweet songs, but actually to make many important discoveries concerning the secret workings of Nature — discoveries which he would never have been impelled to make at all, but for the loving interest which the loss of his Lady had been the first thing to awaken in him. He took Sultan over his seed-beds and laboratories to show him how far he had carried this, and as he stood beside one of his experiments, explaining its meaning to his visitor in the most courteous manner and the most graceful phrases imaginable, Sultan could not help losing himself in admiration of the man.

Every tone, every gesture, every chance fold of his beautiful and dignified garments seemed to betray how well the Poet realised what a noble figure, what a grand old man, the Poet looked!

"And the lady herself," Sultan enquired tentatively that evening, as they sat once again on the balcony under the stars, "she must have indeed been a wonderful, a glorious creature, to have inspired all this beauty and labour." Tears came into the Poet's eyes, and he nodded, too full of emotion to speak.

"Pardon me if it is painful," went on Sultan gently, "but may I know … when … how long ago did she die?"

"She is not dead!" said the Poet.

"I see!" said Sultan. "She refused … she loved another!"

"No! No!" explained the Poet quickly, "you have misunderstood. It was I who refused *her*!" Sultan looked at his host with bewilderment.

"Ah, I see!" said the Poet at last, "you have not yet grown out of those bourgeois notions that I also found so troublesome at the time."

"I am sorry, Sir!" said Sultan humbly. "I confess I *had* misunderstood. You spoke of the parting — of fate … of longings …" The Poet nodded.

"A time came," he explained affably, "when I felt (it was inevitable) that we no longer had a living, *concrete* relation!" He waved his hand. "You have doubtless read my little tale of the man who married the pygmy maiden? She had never understood me, and indeed how could I expect her to?"

"But if she had never understood …"

"What is love?" said the Poet in his low, rich, musical voice. "The poet sees in the maiden — the Almighty and his Angels and all his wide Universe! And the maiden sees in the poet — what? A mystery which she does not fully comprehend, which she is incapable of comprehending, of which she is, however, prettily proud! and which ennobles her with the bewildering sense of her own unworthiness. The Dove has alighted on her for an instant and she trembles, and wonders why!"

Sultan was silent. For some reason all the terrible sorrow and loneliness, which the Poet's conversation had succeeded for a time in soothing, now returned upon him with redoubled force.

"I wonder," he said to the Poet at last, musingly, "if you have ever tasted the taste of ashes?"

"I fear I do not understand!" said the Poet. "Ashes! Certainly not! Why should I have done?"

Sultan did not reply, but, after a pause, announced his intention of leaving on the following day, in order to travel further Westward. He intended, he said, to call on the Philosopher. On hearing this, the Poet laughed with jovial condescension.

"That mole!" he exclaimed.

"I have been advised to call," said Sultan, "by those whom I trust and, with your permission, I will do so."

"Certainly!" said the Poet, "you are free to do exactly as you choose. Each one of us should follow his own bent and develop his own capacities to the fullest degree. That is the whole secret of life. As for the Philosopher, he is quite harmless — an excellent fellow. Only," (and he

winked) "he has one or two bats in the belfry on the matter
of — telescopes. He thinks, for example, that they are a
cure for blindness! Indeed, I am told that a telescope held
to a blind eye is one of his favourite symbols!"

Sultan thanked the Poet from the depths of his heart for
all his hospitality and kindness, but still more for those treasures
of wisdom and beauty which he had bestowed upon him with
such studied generosity. And the Poet took these compliments
and expressions of gratitude, as he took everything that came
his way, with the most graceful air in the world.

"And now," he said heartily to his guest. "I will give you
something good to take away with you!" and fetching his
lyre he sang to Sultan in his beautiful tenor voice the very
latest sonnet which he had composed. It was something
like this, only wiser and more musical: –

Had they but told me that her name is Sleep,
How many pangs of sorrow had been saved!
Whose secret lovers neither watch nor weep,
Being by her kisses wondrously enslaved!
Had they but told me, none need lie forlorn
Since icy Death was swallowed up in love,
And how Sleep's sunny breasts are fields of corn
Through which each lover walks with his first love!
Had they but told — Ah veils of fragrant blue,
Open! Ah, hold me close, close to thy breast!
Oh warm lips! Breath that maketh old life new,
Shall mouth not sing that on this mouth was pressed?
   Love, love, how many eyes will cease to weep,
   When I shall tell them that thy name is Sleep!

The Poet's voice died away under the stars, and the vibrating strings of the lyre fell reluctantly silent. Deeply moved, Sultan once more thanked him humbly for all that he had done and said. He then retired to rest and early next morning, before his host was astir, left the peaceful homestead and continued his journey, bearing the sonnet with him securely locked in his memory.

He travelled Westward for many weeks, and gradually it became clear to him that he was penetrating farther and farther into the dominion of Abdol. For by day the sky was darkened with the smoke of Abdol's factories and by night it blazed with his blast-furnaces or glared and twitched with garish electrical panegyrics of his proprietary monopolies. It was full Autumn when at last, in the centre of a dirty town, one of a row in a mean street behind a huge gasometer, whose aroma pervaded the soot-blackened air week in week out, he found the Philosopher's dwelling. There cannot anywhere, thought Sultan to himself, as soon as he set eyes on the Philosopher, be a man more different than this from the Poet. His clothes — a shabby old coat and a pair of sagging cylindrical trousers — hung loosely from his rounded shoulders; his voice was loud and startling; all his movements were boyish and awkward and, as if not contented with the quality of soot which descended steadily from Abdol's chimneys alike on himself and on the squalid children playing in the gutter, he must needs pour a perpetual column of it into the air from a tobacco-pipe which was itself no less than a small chimney.

There appeared at first to be one point only in which he resembled the Poet — and that was the instant unhesitating hospitality with which he welcomed Sultan to his house. As to the conversation, that was indeed different from what it had been with the Poet. The two never spoke openly of Love or Sorrow, and the Philosopher, when he did reveal his private sentiments, preferred to do so in a curious roundabout way by means of sly jokes at his own expense (often so complicated that Sultan failed to understand them) and remarks of a kind which seemed on the surface to imply that he, the Philosopher, was of all insignicant people in the world perhaps the most insignificant. Sultan could not help noticing, however, that for all the Philosopher's personal reticence, he felt, before he had been with him for very long, a warmer current of sympathy for himself than he had ever done when he was with the Poet. Nevertheless it troubled him a great deal that they could never open their hearts to one another in the ordinary simple way.

At last, one day, the Philosopher had just been making one of these sly, good-humoured jests at his own expense. This time it turned on his poverty. Sultan deliberately turned the conversation by taking him seriously and gravely commiserating with him that a man of such intellectual dignity should be obliged to live so meanly. The Philosopher at once became uneasy. He began to quip and quibble and jest more furiously than ever. Yet Sultan, by dint of still taking everything he said in deadly earnest, at last *forced* him too to be serious, and in this way elicited from him a part at any rate of his life-story. It appeared that the reason of his being so poor was that no less than three-quarters of his income went to the support

of an imbecile lady, who, just before the misfortune which
turned her brain, had been betrothed to him! For
apparently, in spite of the disaster which now separated
them in space, the Philosopher regarded himself as
irrevocably wedded to her!

Greatly shocked, Sultan expressed his solicitude that his
friend should be obliged to support all the obligations
without experiencing any of the blessings of matrimony.

"Why, as to that, Sir!" replied the Philosopher in his
curiously loud and startling voice: "as it is necessarily
determined largely by accident, so to the Philosopher it is
a matter of comparative indifference *which* particular
woman he shall select as the recipient of his homage.
What does import is that, when once the eclectic faculty
has been exercised, that homage shall be lifelong. Sir, he
is not to deny the *existence* of the Pleasures and Pains of
Affection, but neither, on the other hand, is he to allow
them any weight in the reckoning by which he determines
his public actions!"

Sultan, looking at the calm and stoical mask of a face,
through which the Philosopher uttered these words, found
himself quite unable to determine how much this man
really suffered from his calamities. All he could say for
certain was that the comfort and assurance which he had
formerly derived from the Poet were as nothing to the
comfort which he felt when he contemplated — not so
much the Philosopher himself as the fact that such a man
was to be found in such a place.

He stayed many weeks with the Philosopher and they
had many delightful conversations concerning the Life of

Reason, in the course of which the Philosopher expounded his doctrine that Reason, which amid the Many ever holds fast to the One, arises solely out of Constancy and is only to be sustained by that virtue.

These conversations were greatly to Sultan's taste, and he would probably have stayed longer still, had it not been for a certain foible of his host's of which the Poet had warned him, and which towards the end of his stay acted on Sultan so powerfully that it began to make him ill. In the centre of the tiny, smoke-blackened yard which he insisted on referring to as his 'garden', mounted on a large steel tripod, there stood — dearest to the Philosopher of all his few possessions — a large telescope. He had an insatiable passion for star-gazing. This would have mattered little to his guest, had it not been for the odd way in which the Philosopher's astronomical proclivities reacted on his whimsical flair for emphasising his own insignificance — and that of mankind in general. As it was, nearly ever fine night, when they had come in from the garden, he would immediately begin reading Sultan a long, fantastic, and intolerably tedious lecture about all that they had seen through the telescope.

"You remember that very bright star we saw above the Gasometer?" he would say, as they sat together over the fire. And Sultan would nod sleepily.

"Well, are you aware that if you drove a sixty horse-power engine from here to that star, it would take you five hundred and forty-five quadrillion, nine thousand million billion trillion, two billion, six hundred thousand seven hundred and thirty-three million, four hundred and forty-four thousand five hundred and one years to get there?"

"No, I was not aware of that!" Sultan would reply, and he would make a gesture to show that he was suitably impressed.

"So that on the whole," the Philosopher would continue, stretching out his legs with great satisfaction towards the blaze, "I do not think we need trouble to *try* and get there — eh?"

Once or twice something in the Philosopher's attitude on these occasions suggested to Sultan that his host's secret and besetting sin might be *laziness*! And the longer he stayed, the more convinced did he become of this. It seemed to throw a new and less favourable light on that curious love of stressing his own smallness and insignificance — for after all, if you are too small to do anything, what need is there to stir!

It would all have been comparatively unimportant, had not Sultan's nature been such an impressionable one. As it was, everything the Philosopher said had its peculiar effect on him, an effect which was never greater than on one strange evening, when the latter's sense of his own insignificance suddenly changed for a few moments into its opposite. On this occasion, after speaking at great length to Sultan, and with the usual tedious quantity of figured illustration, about the enormous distances of stars from the earth, he suddenly looked up and, striking an attitude which corresponded in an odd way to that of the steel tripod, shook his fist at the firmament! He then turned to Sultan, who realised for the first time that he was not jesting but in deadly earnest.

"Man is only truly man," he cried, "when he can stand four-square to the Universe, as I am standing now, and hurl defiance at its icy ruthlessness, even as I am hurling it now!" And again he shook his bony fist at the sky.

Sultan looked at the Philosopher and then at the starry sky behind him. It could not be denied that the scene was impressive. The very ludicrousness and pathos of the Philosopher's figure made it more so. Nor had Sultan himself spent all these long evenings looking through the telescope without some result. The night sky did really look very different to him now from what it had looked as it hung low and love-breathing over the seraglio or unrolled its secret wisdom to the open heart of the Temple. How cold it looked to-night! How empty! How indifferent to that very 'constancy' of the Philosopher's which it so much resembled! Sultan shivered. The Philosopher's own figure no longer looked ludicrous in his eyes but dignified — commanding — tall. He seemed to have fallen under its spell.

And then a strange thing happened. For some moments Sultan's unquiet gaze had been resting more particularly on the great star Sirius, which stood now over the Eastern horizon, flaming forth into the blackness its brilliant and penetrating green. Suddenly, and only for an instant of time, the green turned to a no-less brilliant orange, and then immediately the colour was again as before. He rubbed his eyes. There was no denying it. The Dog-Star had winked at him! And now he looked once more at the Philosopher and this time, as he did so, made quiet involuntarily a noise which the Philosopher himself had, with great difficulty, taught him to make. He laughed.

"Come along," he said, laying his hand familiarly on his host's shoulder. "We shall get cramp if we go on standing four-square too long. Let us go in!"

The Philosopher gave him a curious look.

"Perhaps I was a little carried away just now," he said after a time, rather diffidently. Sultan made no reply, but shortly afterwards he announced his intention of leaving next day. He thanked his host even more warmly than he had thanked the Poet for his hospitality.

"Which way shall you go?" asked the Philosopher quickly in order to interrupt his effusions.

"Westward!" said Sultan.

"But you *cannot*!" exclaimed the Philosopher. "There *is* no Westward from here!" Sultan looked at him, wondering if he had taken leave of his senses, and the Philosopher, seeing that he was disbelieved, became excited.

"Yes," he said, nodding his head. "It is *proved*! As soon as you get beyond that Gasometer (and here he pointed to the Gasometer just behind his own little house) as soon as you get beyond that Gasometer, you are knocked on the head invisibly from behind and dragged violently into a certain vortex, or complex of forces, which is now known to be an Etheric Retort. After a short interval the Etheric Retort spins you out backwards into the Fourth Dimension. When you finally recover consciousness, you actually find yourself travelling willy-nilly in an Eastward direction, not Westward as you had intended. So there *is* no Westward. Q.E.D."

Sultan turned his head away to hide the embarrassment which he felt at hearing one who could think so lucidly, when he chose, talking such arrant nonsense.

"Now do you even know what all that means yourself, Philosopher?" he asked patiently.

"No!" replied the Philosopher. "But that is only because I do not happen to have gone into these matters. But I know it is true," he added aggressively, "because those who do specialise in such things have proved it by experiments showing that light has hiccoughs!" And once again Sultan had to turn away his head in order to hide his deep and painful blush.

That evening, as they sat together, Sultan realised that it was for the last time. His heart warmed to the Philosopher and, acting on an impulse, he confided in him at last the secret of his great loss. When he had finished speaking the Philosopher, continuing to look into the fire and speaking in a studiously detached tone, replied:

"I am not the less touched by your confidence, my dear Sir, because I had as a matter of fact already guessed that the Absolute has recently chosen to appear to you — as indeed it appears at some time or other to most of us — in the form on an attractive young female."

"Ah," said the Sultan, who liked the tone of the Philosopher's voice much better than he liked his words. "You are now saying something the same kind of thing as the Poet said to me. It is the first time since I have been here, that that has happened."

"I should not have thought," replied his host, "that senile decay was upon me so soon! Please explain yourself!" And he snorted contemptuously.

"Well," replied Sultan hesitatingly, "you would comfort

me if I understood you aright, by pointing out that my —
my misery is but a temporary illusion?"

"Not at all," replied the Philosopher. "One part of
appearance is no more illusory than another, and if the
Absolute appears in the form of a young female — well,
then, it appears in that form! It may suit us, in the dearth
of words, to speak of love as if the Absolute had played
us a sort of trick, dressing up as a girl, so to speak, and
hiding its Gorgon stare behind a pair of sparkling eyes, in
order to be able to look at us without turning us
immediately to stone. But in fact, of course, the Absolute
plays no tricks."

"It is all very fine," complained the Sultan dismally, "but
unfortunately it is not the Absolute that I am missing at
the moment."

"Then what is it?"

"It is simply Lady, Sir — Lady *herself*!"

To these words, which Sultan had cried out in despair,
the Philosopher replied kindly but firmly, and in a tone of
voice which made Sultan feel half ashamed of himself: –

"I am afraid that is flat blasphemy! As to your so-called
Romance, we are to value it of course; but we are to value
it in its proper light — *sub specie aeternitatis*. No one but
a fool would *continue* trying to value the young female *herself*
— the mere objective personality — any the more highly
for what had occurred." Sultan was silent.

The following morning he took his leave, after wringing
his host's hand and thanking him warmly again and again
for all his hospitality and personal kindness. The Philosopher
followed him out into the street and stood there for a long

time, bareheaded, while he tried once more by means of a well-constructed discourse to convince his guest that it was impossible to travel further westward than he had come already. Sultan listened politely, though he knew well that the Philosopher might argue both of them asleep without convincing him or deterring him one iota from making the attempt. The confusion of the whole scene was enhanced by the fact that one of the children playing in the dirty gutter had just hurt himself in some small way and begun to cry. When the two noises, the loud voice of the Philosopher and the loud crying of the little boy, had been going on for some time together, Sultan ventured to interrupt.

"Cannot we do something about it?" he asked. The Philosopher turned for a moment and looked at the child.

"The Absolute beginning to appear to another of us in the form of sorrow!" he said, in jesting reference to last night's conversation.

"That is no reason for not offering consolation!" said Sultan, quickly, and he began to move towards the child.

"A just rebuke!" replied the Philosopher, catching him by the arm and detaining him, "But consider! We have to seek always the greatest good of the greatest number. Now this (and he jerked his head in the direction of the still weeping child) must occur, on a general reckoning, many millions of times a day. I refuse therefore to admit any question but that it is *far* more important for our investigation of the truth not to be interrupted than for the world-total of infantile lacrimation to be reduced by a nominal percentage."

"In any case," replied Sultan, "we are forestalled!" He

was right. While the Philosopher was speaking, a pair of lovers, walking hand in hand, had come up with the crying little boy. The woman at once stooped and, picking him up in her arms, kissed him, whilst the man felt in his pocket and gave him a penny. Sultan stood watching the scene. When at last the two went on again, the little boy had ceased crying and was turning the penny over and over in his hand with a doubtful look. Turning to the Philosopher, to shake hands once more and take his leave, Sultan fancied that he looked a little uncomfortable. He himself was surprised to find how this little incident had helped to lighten the load of sorrow which he felt at leaving so true a friend.

IV

As HE HAD expected, Sultan experienced none of the alarming adventures which the Philosopher had predicted for him. He passed the Gasometer and continued trudging further and further westward without suffering anything more violent than the augmentation of his loneliness. This in itself however, was terrible enough. With every step which he took towards the setting sun, solitude seemed to thicken around him like a winding-sheet. The very people he encountered on the way looked increasingly foreign, increasingly remote, increasingly wrapped up in their own unhealthy dreams. Not only had he now no more friends to call on, but his supply of money was running low. Day after day passed without his speaking to a soul, unless it were the scolding thin-faced women who kept the squalid lodgings in which he was obliged to spend his nights, and whose sour complexions were the first thing on which his eyes opened in the mornings.

He found, too, that the Philosopher's astronomical aberrations had taken much deeper effect on him than he had supposed at the time. For, whereas formerly, when night came on and the stars twinkled out into the soft and velvety blackness, he had been used to perceive, on looking up, the magical dance of Shiva, as he passed from star to star weaving his shining web and transforming the whole heavens into a rich embroidered robe for the Beloved, now he could perceive nothing in the sky but so many glittering steely points of light set at distance from one another, as if punched in ebony.

One evening, not long after he left the Philosopher, his lonely and sorrowing heart peeped for comfort through his eyes, only to dash itself once more in vain against the hostile glittering array; and this time such an unspeakable mournfulness descended on him that he was on the point of fainting. Yet in that very moment it came to him as if in a dream that the stars themselves were perhaps after all not icy, indifferent, metallic, as they looked, that they would indeed have liked, instead of piercing his heart, to bend down to it with soft whispers of comfort, but that some spell held them rigid in their places. And the sadness of that spell seemed to come echoing down out of the firmament to him, so that he heard the westering stars singing to one another in faint and helpless voices words which sounded something like this:—

Alack, what empty leagues of space!
What galaxies of sightless eyes!
Through what steel chain of nights and days
We rise and south and set and rise!
Islanded in despair, alone,
The westering pilgrim seeks his own.

All through the night the thin dirge of the lonely stars rang on through Sultan's dreams and all the next day its echo was the background of his mood, which grew heavier and heavier as he passed on. And now everything about him added to his unhappiness. For, with his further progress westward, he had come into an uglier country than he had ever seen in his life before. Everything was

Abdol's. In the towns the gasometers were not one or two, placed here and there, but clustering as thick as trees in a grove; and the smoking factories were so many and so close to one another that he was never out of the sound of the grinding of their wheels; and the population was so numerous that he seemed to be always wading through drifting streams of white faces — white, weary, coarse, expressionless faces, white faces, white faces, chattering white faces.

Even the so-called country between the towns now bristled everywhere with sharp-pointed steel or concrete posts, on which spidery cables ran to and fro and back again, as if laughing at the worn and littered patches of grass beneath them, that had once been green fields.

Evening came on once more and with its coming Sultan's heart seemed to break. 'If only I could sing!' he thought, 'like the Poet!' But when he remembered all the wonderful things which the Poet had said about love, he felt abashed, for *he* had only one thought and that was Lady herself. And when he remembered all the learned things the Philosopher had said about love, his heart dried up within him, and he felt that he was fit for nothing but to be laughed at. He looked up again at the stars and, as he did so, realised that the night was drawing on, so that he must once more seek lodging. And then Sultan suddenly bethought him of the cold, empty, fireless room in which he would surely have to sleep and of the sour-faced landlady who would awaken him in the morning with some sarcastic complaint that he was staying longer than the time he had paid for, and all his great longing for Lady and all

that he had suffered and all that the weary white faces
drifting past him all day must have suffered before they
came to look so weary, so dull and so white, all these things
suddenly sprang together in Sultan's heart, took fire, and
leaped up in a single pure flame, so that he opened his
mouth and, almost without knowing it, began singing: —

I have been very lonely all to-day,
Above the million voices of the crowd
Hearing one voice I might not set at bay
Of lost imagination, crying loud
How wide the world was it must wander through
And for what empty years — till in dismay
I turned mine eyes up to the stars and knew
Only that they were very far away.
 Ah, God, to come this evening to some room
 And, dropping soft the latch on stars and men,
 To find my Lady in its firelit gloom
 Filling it with her loveliness, and then
 To take her in my arms and hear her say:
 "I have been very lonely all to-day!"

Sultan felt wonderfully comforted by this song of his. It
seemed to him to warm his heart again — perhaps even to
warm the stars. And the next day he came to that part of
the country which he had all along been seeking, a
peninsular on the West Coast, shaped like a triangle and
called Delta. The westernmost point of this peninsular,
whither Sultan arrived in the early afternoon, was formed
by a single huge triangular mass of crystalline rock that

towered high above the Pacific Ocean, into which its apex jutted. This rock was called Cape Limit. Now Sultan had often heard the Philosopher and his friends talking glibly about this peninsular, of which most of them had a set of the neatest imaginable maps. The Poet, too, had spoken of the place, but without much interest. As for the Philosopher, he used actually to employ his map for the purpose of calculating the enormous distances of the stars, both from each other and from the earth. But although they possessed these maps, they had all agreed that it was impossible to actually *visit* the peninsular, which they said was not merely a wild uninhabited place, but positively inaccessible. Even if it should be possible to struggle as far as the actual peninsular — so they had all told him (and there would be nothing to see, when you arrived!) — there was still not the slightest doubt of its being absolutely unthinkable that any living person should reach Cape Limit itself.

All this passed through Sultan's mind, as he stood this afternoon on the western-most tip of the high promontory and looked out to sea. It was a strange afternoon all lost in a uniform light haze as smooth as mother-of-pearl. Sea and sky merged indistinguishably together at the invisible horizon and the strong black rock on which he stood seemed to be the only separate object in the world.

There was no ship in sight nor any tiniest ripple on the surface of the sea beneath him. A lonely figure, carven, like the rock on which he stood, out of the mysterious grey void, Sultan stood motionless for some minutes, gazing Westward — minutes which he was never to forget through all the rest of his life.

At last he turned back from the cliff, and he smiled to himself, as he perceived that, so far from the whole peninsular being uninhabited, even the rocky Cape possessed a commodious-looking hotel. Some day, he said to himself, perhaps the Philosopher will come and see for himself! This hotel, which was a round building with a small glass cupola at the top, looked singularly well-suited to the barren headland on which it had been built, and Sultan felt an overwhelming desire to spend a night in it. After enquiring at the door and counting the money in his pocket, he found that he had just enough left to enable him to do so. It would cost him his very last penny. What he should do and whither he should turn the following morning, he had as yet no idea; but he decided in this particular case to let the future take care of itself.

Sultan was surprised, on entering the hotel, to find that such an attractive and even beautiful building was the work and property of no other than the great Abdol himself! Everything else of Abdol's which he had ever seen, had positively hurt him with its ugliness. Here everything appeared to be just as it should be; not only was the exterior attractive, but every fitting, every article of furniture within the building was ideally shaped and adapted to its purpose. Even the name which Abdol had chosen for his hotel, instead of being one of those mis-spelt polyglot inventions of which he was usually so fond, was a pleasant one, not without certain antique associations about it. It was called *The Saracen's Head*.

Sultan himself was the only guest, and, when he retired to bed, he was surprised to find that he had been put to sleep at the very top of the house, in a room under the glass cupola. The cupola was in fact his only window, nor did he need any other, since it was so large as to form the whole of the roof and the greater part of the walls of his circular chamber. Sultan was rather distressed to find that no curtains had been provided, yet he did not feel disposed to ask for them. Having undressed himself, therefore, he lay down on the bed and, looking upward, at once perceived that he was exposed through the glass dome to the whole vault of the starry firmament. He shivered a little beneath the merciless steel glitter of its downward gaze, and after a time turned his face to the West, where the mist over the ocean still shrouded some few of the million points of light in a softer and more earthly mystery. For a long while he tossed and turned on the bed in a vain endeavour to forget his hot and aching temples and fall asleep. But it was of no avail. At last, turning once more towards the silvery mist, he bethought him of the song which he had sung to himself on the previous day and, as he did so, his eyes closed for an instant, and at once a vision of the Holy One stood before him. Clad in a simple white robe, she seemed to advance towards him smiling and holding out a scroll and, as she unfastened the scroll to spread it before him, his eyes opened and he was awake; but not before he had realised that the scroll contained written on it the words of the sonnet which the Poet had sung to him on the eve of his departure from his house.

Comforted and partly strengthened by this dream-vision of his Lady, Sultan abandoned his attempts to escape from the glare of the stars and lay on his back instead, staring calmly up at them. Very softly now he began murmuring over to himself the words of the Poet's sonnet and, as he did so, his heart grew warmer and his head grew cooler and his blood began to tingle with the sweetest drowsiness. In the last moment before he closed his eyes, it seemed to Sultan that the stars had come down nearer to him and that he was to give himself up to them with the same mystic abandonment as that which he had once used towards his wives in the seraglio.

In the middle of the night, Sultan was aroused by the crowing of cocks and the barking of watchdogs. Turning quickly to the East, he observed that Sirius was rising into view over the sill of the glass dome, which formed the roof of his chamber. Never had Sultan seen the Dog-Star flare and flash with such brilliancy and such violence. And as he lay there in the pleasant visionary mood betwixt sleeping and waking — that mood in which what is without seems often as if it were within, and what is within without — he gradually became aware that the furious star was singing. Sultan bent his ear attentively to the words, anxious to miss no more of them than he must have missed already, and he was only just in time; for the Song of Sirius was all but done. What he heard seemed to add to the dreamlike confusion of his mood, for at one moment it came to him as strange and new and then at another, as if he had heard it all before, a long time ago, far back in his childhood — had heard it spoken in the very same words. Was it a laugh or a bark? Was it this, after all, which had awakened him, and not the barking of earthly watchdogs? Hark! –

Ha! Ha! Wow wow wow!
Ha! Ha! Wow wow wow!
　The sky grows paler in the east,
　The strains of strutting chanticleer
　Awaken bird and sleeping beast:
　Mortal awake! Thy dawn is near.
Ha! Ha! Wow wow wow!
　The time is near: the tube forsaken lies:
　Immortal mortals wake and use your eyes!

And then, just before the voice of the singing star died
away into silence, there came, more clearly than before,
that echo out of the past which he found so bewildering.
The old words, the very words almost without alteration,
which he had learnt at school; but their *meaning* seemed
to have altered completely! It was as if he had only been
dreaming when he heard them before and was now at last
awake:

　Else a great Prince in prison dies!

The voice of Sirius faded away. Sultan looked up,
through the crown of the dome, into the zenith. He was
astonished to observe that it was now quite a different sky
from that under which he had fallen asleep. The blackness
and the iron glitter had vanished; instead the face of the
heavens was all a stabbing violet depth wherefrom the
million twinklings of the stars seemed quite naturally to
draw their more visible points of radiance. No longer was

the space between them empty, but as if it, too, were composed of uninterrupted star-stuff. And it was full of throbbings and workings and these throbbings and workings were themselves the violet hue of the interstellar profundity. And as he fixed his eyes on the seven great stars of the Bear, these throbbings and workings, which had drawn together at the seven points into the seven stars, seemed to him to begin boiling and seething more violently, until at last they issued from the depths above him in the form of a harmony of voices, which sang to him as if taking up all that Sirius had left unfinished:

Quick! Thou shalt see the subtle bands
Twixt star and star — the throbbing wires,
As we march singing hands in hands,
In joyous companies and choirs.

Sultan gazed and gazed. He thought he had never heard or seen anything so terrifying or so sweet. "Quick!" went on singing the seven stars of the Great Bear,

Quick! Ere they fade! Through clefts in time
The waking sleeper's eye doth climb –

And then, at the end of the song of the Great Bear, followed yet another of those mysterious echoes which took Sultan back to his childhood, and with such force that he even half forgot the present and seemed to be living both parts of his life at the same moment:

Higher than the sphery chime!

By now the violet depths of the firmament had broken up into a riot of various colour, through the midst of which, like a magical and fragrant zone, the unbroken chain of the great Ecliptic, interwoven of hues yet more brilliant and of forms yet more harmoniously blended than all the rest, arched its majestic way. And as he still looked and listened, the constellations of which the Zodiac was composed seemed also to be singing, but more to themselves, and after their own graver and sublimer mood:

Unturning, His disciples turn
In mystic dance about the Sun
(He sent us forth but to return!)
Weaving the Many into One.
Though numberless as blades of grass,
Each part into the Whole doth pass.

And again that mysterious echo from the past:

Through us! Life is a dome of many-coloured glass!

Sultan awoke with a start. For his previous awakening had been but an awakening within the dream. "A dome of many-coloured glass!" he cried, snatching wildly at the skirts of the fast-fading vision, "then it was the cupola that was coloured and not the heavens!" And at the thought his heart turned to stone within him. And yet, when his waking eyes looked upward, they beheld, as before, only a dome of clear, transparent, colourless glass and the sparkling ebon sky beyond it. Whence then, had the vision of colour come to him? Was it gone for ever? Ah, solitude, solitude more unbearable than ever!

He turned again to the East, as if to implore the Dog-star to sing to him again and thus begin a second vision, but to his surprise the Dog-star was no longer there. For it was no longer midnight as in his dreamed awakening, but nearing dawn. And now, not far above the eastern horizon, slowly ascending and filling, as she did so, the vaulted firmament with the bounty of her outstretched wings, there stood before him the glorious constellation of the Virgin. Sultan gazed and gazed, and at last, out of the desolation of his awakening to reality he stretched forth forlorn arms, as if praying to her for help. And behold, his prayer was answered. For once more the paling sky began to throb betwixt the stars, there was a mysterious circulation as of invisible blood, and at the same time the great lifeless "Y" melted into a breathing woman, a fair woman, a divine woman, who stooped for an instant from the sky and folded over his heart the benison of her softest and most loving wings.

In a moment the vision was gone, yet in the compass of that moment Sultan knew such security, such bliss, and such high courage as he had only once before in his life even dreamed of — and that was when Lady had taken him in her arms and kissed him on the night before she was lost to him for ever. Once more now he was staring through the empty glass at the constellation hovering above him and, as her form faded back into the great lifeless "Y", the voice of the Virgin seemed to echo faintly in his ears, mingling confusedly with those of her neighbours in the Zodiac. It was a sweet clear soprano voice:

But my wings folded o'er a heart –

it sang, and, as soon as it began singing, other voices broke in on it, making it difficult to follow through the maze of sound, which was nevertheless (could one but trace it out) a wonderfully sweet harmony.

And he who struggles never fails

broke in the other voices, two voices, singing together, and Sultan could not tell whence they came. And then he heard the Virgin's voice again, continuing her own song, and mingled with it a fourth and deeper voice, uttering the same words with her in unison:

Teach it to play the Lion's part!

while the other two voices went on, also taking up their theme:

Out of the Scorpion through the Scales.

till at last all four voices joined together and at the same time others seemed to come to their aid, as if the whole firmament were singing, and immediately all the voices died away, yet not till after Sultan had heard them all sing to him in earnest unison:

Oh, traveller through the Zodiac
Pass further on — by turning back!

The voices died away and the vision vanished. It was full dawn. Sultan lay watching the stars vanish one by one into the grey, quietly, like the candles in the Temple after the priests and the singers have departed. He saw nothing now but the empty glass dome and the blank walls of his room. But his heart was at peace. For he had hope, and he knew what he must do.

V

WHEN HE HAD breakfasted next morning and paid his score, Sultan no longer had a penny in his pocket. The whole store of wealth which he had brought with him from Asia had given out. He knew now where he wished to go; but how was he to live? The difficulty resolved itself in an unexpected way. As he was about to leave the hotel, the manager called him aside and presented him with a little metal object.

"A souvenir of your stay in the hotel!" he said. Sultan would have handed it back to him for a worthless toy, but the fellow insisted that he must take it.

"Mr. Abdol's own special orders!" he said. "Everyone who stops here is given one. Of course you can throw it away, when you get outside, if you choose. That's not my affair. But, if you take my advice, you will keep tight hold of it! For if ever you find yourself with empty pockets — you may find it will enable you to support yourself."

"*Support* myself!" exclaimed Sultan incredulously.

"Yes!" said the hotel-keeper. "Just look at it a minute. What would you say it is?" Sultan turned it over in his hand.

"It is a little model of the peninsular," he said, "with Cape Limit at one end and a tiny round hole at the point to represent the Hotel."

"Nothing else?" asked the man.

"It seems to be very much the same thing as my friend the Philosopher possessed. A sort of map. Only it is made of steel and his was made of paper!"

"Nothing else?" Sultan shook his head.

"It is a key," said the hotel-keeper.

"Well, I still do not understand how it will support me!"

"In these parts," explained the innkeeper, "the people are growing terribly absent-minded. They seem to lose their heads more and more every day. The result is that there is now scarcely a family which has not somewhere in the house a locked door or drawer, of which the key has been accidentally lost, so that the contents are no longer accessible to them. Now your key is a master-key. I might almost call it the master of masters. I doubt if you will find a lock *anywhere* that it will not open, if you only have a little patience. You understand? People will be grateful. They will pay you!"

"And is it a free gift?" asked Sultan. "I have no money to give you for it."

"Absolutely! A free gift from Mr. Abdol himself."

"Yes. That is just what I find so difficult to understand. I have always looked on Abdol as a hard man."

"So he is, and his gift is hard steel. The very hardest. There is a special process. It will stand anything!"

"But why does he *give* it away?" The innkeeper shrugged his shoulders.

Sultan left the hotel and began, according to the plan which he had formed early in the morning, to retrace his steps exactly over the route by which he had come. The innkeeper was quite right. Although he no longer had any money left out of his own inheritance, he found no difficulty whatever in obtaining a livelihood. The people were delighted with the travelling locksmith, and it was moreover pleasant work; for it was always the drawers containing the things they valued most which they asked him to open. And it would very often happen that they themselves had forgotten how delightful these old possessions were. "I had quite forgotten how lovely it is!" the old women would exclaim, as they drew forth, perhaps their bridal dresses laid carefully away in lavender years and years ago. And on one occasion Sultan left behind him a rubicund, gouty old gentleman playing happily with a toy which he had not seen since he was six years old.

Sultan was particularly surprised to notice that the coin with which his customers paid him was of a new pattern, stamped, not as formerly with the head of the Lord of Albion, but actually with the head of Abdol himself. For fear of offending them, however, he forebore for the time being to ask any questions.

He continued steadily retracing his steps and, as he passed the place of their abode, called in for a few hours on both the Philosopher and the Poet. Both were delighted to see him, congratulated him on his healthy appearance, and — refused to believe that he had been to Cape Limit, or even to Delta! The Philosopher assured him that he had no unopened drawers, though Sultan knew, from his last visit, that this was untrue. As a matter of fact, the Philosopher was so absentminded that he had forgotten the existence of the very drawers, let alone their contents. The latter also assured him with much sly humour that his steel key was *only a copy made from the paper map*! Nevertheless they parted very good friends.

At last Sultan came back to Albion, and in time back to the city of the terrible disaster. He wondered very much if the palace had been rebuilt, what its appearance was and who lived in it; and, although he arrived in the town after dark, made his way immediately towards the centre of the town, where the Palace grounds were situated. Many and great changes had occurred. Where the great wrought-iron gates had stood, dividing the cool and peaceful darkness of the Palace gardens from the garish night life of the town, there was now only a gaudy wooden framework, something like the proscenium of a theatre. This was lit up with a chaotic profusion of parti-coloured electric bulbs, above the top of which stood in enormous illuminated letters the words

FUN FAIR

and beneath, in letters not much smaller,

ABDOL'S GREAT GIFT TO A GREAT NATION.

Inside, it was brighter than day. Strings of electric bulbs were slung to and fro from posts, dotted here and there about the littered ground, while still taller posts, square monsters of latticed steel, upheld great arc lamps whose carbons, crackling continually, flooded the ground beneath them with a bluish glare. Hammer-blows, shrieks of laughter, the hooting of sirens, an incessant blare of steam-organs, playing different tunes, hoarse voices raised in advertisement and in dispute, all these things combined to fill the air with an indescribable din which made Sultan's heart sink within him, so that he felt he could not go a step further. He looked desperately round him for some more familiar sight. Ah! Not far away, a little more softly illuminated than the remainder of the buildings in the fair, stood a large concrete building which bore in tall letters standing up along its roof-ridge the inscription

ABDOL'S PALACE OF DANCING.

Gentle memories began to stir in Sultan's breast; and there was something restful in the lighting of the place which appealed to the tender melancholy they brought with them. He approached the building, and for the first time in his life, he paid money in order to enter a ball-room.

But, once inside, he was glad he had come. No one, it is true, was dancing and there was no music playing, but this could only mean an interval between two numbers. The room itself was dimly yet pleasantly lit with a diffused light, of which the actual source was invisible. The result was a low, romantic twilight, wherein the watery reflections in the highly polished floor moved mysteriously to and fro. Sultan found the subdued illumination very restful to his tired eyes. So low indeed were the lights that it was some little time before he could even see the dancers, who sat, most of them, in little alcoves let into the walls. The alcoves, each of which held a single couple, were shrouded in deep shadow and Sultan observed with pleasure, looming out of the darkness above the heads of each couple, a single romantic red rose. Growing more accustomed to his surroundings, he realised that the couple in the alcove nearest to himself were engaged in conversation. It was the girl who was speaking and, in spite of himself, Sultan overheard her words. She was saying:

"As to what you said just now, if we call the element of intellectual agreement (the psychological minimum datum) X, and the element of pure appetite (the physical minimum datum) Y, then we shall have a very fair idea of the meaning of the question-begging term you introduced just now, as it would be when divested of all its accidental historical and emotive accretions. And that I consider to be absolutely necessary before we can even discuss the question!"

"Certainly," replied the man. "When I say, 'I love you,' then, I mean, X+Y. I mean in the first place that certain specifiable cortical or cuticular – " he suddenly broke off. "Presently!" he added as the two rose to their feet simultaneously. And now Sultan perceived, to his surprise, that what he had at first taken for a rose hanging in the darkness at the back of each alcove was, in fact, nothing else than the two thick lips of an enormous naked negro.[2] The couple, to which he had been listening, had evidently risen in obedience to the command of their particular negro, who now stepped forth from the alcove and, after first showing his teeth in the broadest of broad grins, began to shoot in and out his lips and his posterior simultaneously, ejaculating, as he did so, in a series of explosive bursts:

---

[2] In 1993 Barfield asked the reader to remember that this passage was written "in the unregenerate days before 1930." This passage does not represent his personal view then or ever.

I am de boys
Dat makes no noise:
Hoo! Ha!
Hoo! Ha! Ha!

Meanwhile the man and the girl, standing face to face but without looking at one another, rubbed the front part of their bodies together; after which they turned about and, while the negro repeated his ejaculations, very solemnly rubbed their backs up and down together in the same fashion. The negro then retired to the back of the alcove and the couple resumed their sitting out. Whereupon Sultan heard the girl say:

"The music is getting much better, dear. That was an awfully jolly one." To which the man began to reply:

" – Certain specifiable cuticular reactions would, given the requisite spatial proximity, undoubtedly be effectuated. In the second place I mean to imply …"

But by this time Sultan had moved out of earshot. And after finally satisfying himself that the whole ball was indeed no more than a collection of independent performances of this kind executed by the various couples in accordance with the caprices of their negros, he hurried out of the building by the way he had come.

He began to explore the rest of the Fair. Never in all his travels had he seen such indescribable confusion or heard such an extraordinary racket. Crowds thronged everywhere. Men, women and children jostled one another incessantly and all the more violently owing to the vacant mood in which they were wandering to and fro, uncertain whither to turn next. Sometimes a man or a child would be knocked over and nearly trampled by the aimless crowd; but after a time he would get up on his feet again and go on staring and staring without ever having so much as closed his stupid gaping mouth. Every available inch of the ground was filled with gaudily coloured and brilliantly lit Amusement erections. These were of the most varied description. Sultan noticed first of all the huge Roundabouts. They seemed to be everywhere; and they were no longer of the old-fashioned type fitted with rising and falling wooden horses. Instead of these, great undulating green and purple dragons, their backs painted with spots and their carven faces tortured into every variety of fury, terror and amazement, tore round and round, snorting coloured fires from their nostrils and carrying in their open bellies placid, unsmiling rows of chewing and smoking humanity. There were moreover Watershoots, Switchbacks, Mountain Railways, Witching Waves, Cranes, Towers, Great Wheels, Weighing Machines, Slipping the Slip, Looping the Loop — devices for hoisting, lowering or shoving the human body about in every conceivable direction, at every conceivable speed, devices for giving it every imaginable kind of sensation. In one part of the Fair there stood rows and rows of stereoscopic peepshows, through which, for the payment of a trifling sum, men and women alike could gaze their fill upon the most cunningly devised pornograms. The rows were double, one for the men and one for the women, who stood back to back on the series of little platforms which had been fixed in front of the stereoscopes. The more virile and full-blooded type of customer was then enticed further on, by a large notice which hung, beyond the last of the stereoscopes, over a long row of curtained booths, bearing the mysterious inscription:

ABDOL'S AUTOMATIC TARTS

Each one of these booths, so Sultan discovered, contained an artificially constructed, electrically warmed lay-figure covered over with real human hair and with splendidly smooth human flesh, which had been obtained by a special process from adolescent corpses. The nude automatons were moreover capable of uttering, through a microphone cunningly concealed in the skull, a few simple endearments! They were of both sexes. Outside each booth stood an attendant, an elegant young woman smartly dressed in a masculine uniform with the commissionaire's peaked cap and striped trousers, who invited the customers, took their money, and then watched them contemptuously in. Sultan was surprised to see how natural the uniforms looked on these girls, until he learnt that they all came from a part of the land where it was now compulsory, as a prophylactic measure against a certain horrible disease, for all females to have their breasts amputated at the age of fourteen.

The insides of these booths, admittance to which was a little more expensive, were very sumptuously appointed; everything was so efficiently disposed that many customers did not even bother between entering and leaving, to take their cigarettes out of their mouths. Indeed an automatic machine for delivering cigarettes stood beside each automatic tart. There appeared also to be a certain amount of competition between the individual booths, which were numbered; for many of the attendants had hung up outside their curtains fetching placards, in order to attract customers to their own booths. The placards bore such legends as:

SOCRATES SAID DESIRE IS PAIN!

SWAT THAT CASTRATION COMPLEX!

COME ALONG, OED! MUMMY'S WAITING!

and so forth.

Somewhere or other, either in large letters or in small, printed on the placards, illuminated below the signs, stamped on the metal, the woodwork, or the upholstery, the name of *Abdol* was always to be found. Everything was Abdol's. And indeed, apart from the appointments of the Fair itself, there were huge advertisements everywhere of Abdol's proprietary monopolies. Sultan was positively amazed at their number and variety.

It seemed in some ways such a short time since he had been in Albion before, and already the place was hardly recognisable. For instance, right in the middle of the whole Fair, dominating all the illuminated signs over the Amusement Apparatus and all the other advertisements as well, there arose one single enormous hoarding, bearing a fabulously expensive advertisement of Abdol's last and favourite monopoly. Or perhaps it was not yet quite a monopoly. Just before he left Sultan stood and watched its illuminated mechanical changes through a complete cycle. A human figure, outlined in innumerable electric bulbs, hung on a large cross, picked out of the darkness in the same way. For a few seconds nothing changed, but then, in the darkness underneath, the helmeted figure of a soldier suddenly appeared. A line of lights, kindling one by one, ran up like a caterpillar out of the soldier's hands into the face of the figure on the cross. There was a pause, and then, at the upper end of the long straight line, something like a sponge materialised itself. With four or five grotesque jerks, the figure on the cross shook its head to and fro, as if in refusal. There was another pause. Above the cross a great capital "I" appeared, and following it, at some distance on the right, an "N". And then, after a slightly longer pause than before, the whole inscription completed itself unexpectedly in a single flash:

IT'S NOT ABDOL'S

and a second later the entire sign blotted itself out and on the darkness which it left was written a single inscription in letters thirty feet high:

ABDOL'S VINEGAR!

Sultan had intended to seek out the exact spot in these transformed gardens where the Palace had formerly stood. But he now found that he was tired out, so tired that he could scarcely move another step. He left the Fair, therefore, and without much difficulty, though at the cost of much weary tramping, found out the inn in which he had slept the last time he was in the city and in which he had had the hideous dream and the still more hideous awakening. Mine Host was as communicative as ever. Before Sultan retired to bed that night he had learnt most of what had happened in Albion since his departure. It seemed that the hotelkeeper had been quite mistaken in his estimate of Abdol's character. Of late Abdol had been positively *loading* the people with kindness!

"How did he begin?" asked Sultan.

"At his instigation," replied Mine Host, "and under his guidance, they took the opportunity of the great conflagration to abolish the monarchy and establish the present republic, which is governed by representatives of the people elected by the votes of every citizen over eight years of age. Now, at the very first election, acting on the advice of a popular journal called *The Lollipop*, the new electors unanimously returned Abdol himself as President of the Republic and First Lord of the Treasury in perpetuity. Abdol generously responded by refusing to foreclose on his mortgages on the Palace Gardens, presenting them instead to the nation for use as an Amusement Park for ever. Not content with this, he announced shortly afterwards that, owing to the great wisdom which the nation had shown in combining the two offices of President and Treasury-lord and, he would add, in vesting the functions of than joint office in himself, he now felt able to revise the whole system under which labour was employed in his factories — which was tantamount to saying the system under which labour was employed throughout the country — practically throughout the world. Mr. Abdol then let the nation into a secret. Engines had long ago been invented, he explained, of such efficiency that, in the bulk of his factories, they could replace some two thirds of the human labour at present employed. Hitherto he had thought it wiser *not* to introduce these machines; indeed he *could* not have profitably introduced them. Now everything was different. Their introduction would therefore be begun immediately in all his factories. The wages paid would henceforth be irrespective of the work done, and the problem of unemployment would be solved in the Amusement Park!"

Mine Host was enthusiastic. But Sultan, himself, who had just come from the Amusement Park, went up to bed with a heavy and a fearful heart.

The next morning he returned to the Park, to seek for the exact spot where the Palace had stood. To his surprise he found that the great heap of ashes had actually been left untouched! Only it was now used as every man's rubbish heap, broken bottles, empty tin cans and dirty pieces of paper and cardboard adding an indescribable squalour to its desolation. Indeed it was above this very spot that Abdol had chosen to erect the great hoarding that advertised his vinegar!

VI

THE SUN HAD just set. The great Amusement Park was still comparatively empty. Not far from the Ash-Heap a man and a woman busied themselves with a battered old tin box, turning it over and over between them and apparently trying to open it, until a dark-haired gentleman came up to them and offered, for a small charge, to open it with his master-key. The man and the woman looked at the foreigner and then, looking at one another, winked and burst out laughing.

"Why, it doesn't matter two hoots to us whether we get it open or not!" said the man. "There's nothing in it. It's only — curiosity!" And he swore again: " — curiosity, that's all it is!" he repeated, and he kicked the tin away from him.

"Perhaps you have some old box or drawer at home that I could open for you?" suggested Sultan.

"Say," said the woman, "what particular glass case did they let *you* out of, while the museum was being hoovered? As if we ever locked anything nowadays!"

"Have you nothing at home that you value, then?"

"Stooge!" exclaimed the man disgustedly. "If we have anything valuable we take it to the Bank. Abdol keeps everything for us to-day — and a good job too!"

"The same answer!" murmured Sultan to himself, as he passed wearily on, "always the same answer!" Soon he approached the Ash-Heap and, leaning in the twilight on one of the rotting posts that supported the low wooden rail that ran round it, fell into a weak, unhappy reverie.

Every day now passed in the same manner. He would spend all the morning and afternoon in the Amusement Park trying in vain to earn a little money, and, when evening came, weary of his small success and indeed of everything, he would make his way to the great Ash-Heap and lean wistfully on its railings, gazing blankly at the few forlorn weeds which had found a precarious footing in this desolation, dreaming and dreaming, and wondering hopelessly what he could do. For, unless he could earn more money, it was impossible to carry out his great plan of retracing his steps back to the East, where he had intended to retire for ever into the Temple, to become a religious, and to live alone at peace.

Instead, he was obliged to go on staying with Mine Host, who for the sake of old times was accommodating him very cheaply. Ah, how he hated that Amusement Park! How the stench and the din and the dust and the vapid gigglings on every side sickened him more hideously every day! But there was something more than his disgust that made him hate it, something that made him hate and fear it, too, something which he could not understand, and which plunged him every evening when he stood, as now, by the Ash-Heap, deeper and deeper into the same weak reverie. Try as he might to deceive himself, it was impossible to deny that the atmosphere with which the Amusement Park surrounded him day after day, the single-minded unending pursuit of pleasure on every side, was beginning to work on him in a subtle manner. Yes, it was arousing, deep down in his soul, all sorts of impulses, desires, hopes, all sorts of ancient greeds which until then he had believed to have been stilled for ever by one cooling touch of the constellated Virgin's wings.   Do what he would, Sultan could not prevent alluring memory-visions of the old days in the seraglio, and of the debonair little concubine, from arising and floating before his eyes. It was this that troubled him most sorely of all and made him loathe, as if it were very poison, the Amusement Park and all the people in it.

It was while his mind was full of these unquiet thoughts that Sultan observed for the first time, among the sooty weeds struggling up out of the refuse on the Heap, a garden Rose. It was a sad, spindly-looking object with one dull red knob at the top, yet there was some magic in the twilight which attracted Sultan's attention to it. It was now nearly dark, and many stars had already appeared in the sky. Sultan looked at the flower again. Yes. It was *glowing*! It seemed to be giving forth a light of its own into the dusk! Or was the soft radiance that shone forth from its face no more than the diurnal gift which it had collected from the sun?

Something in the cool of the evening, and in the quiet happy glowing of the lonely Rose suddenly touched Sultan's heart and for a brief instant filled it with a peace which not even the hooting of the sirens and the momently increasing blare of the steam-organs on the roundabouts, could wholly destroy.

"I will not listen to them!" he cried determinedly. "If I have lost the hope of happiness, I have at any rate found Peace. And that is all that the wise are able to find. The rest is illusion. 'The loss of the Beloved,' said the Philosopher, 'is the finding of the Absolute.' And have I not found the Absolute? Have I not wedded the Virgin herself?

Fool! What need to travel further? *I am already there!*"

As he spoke, Sultan strove with all his might to call up
before his mind's eye in all its tranquil majesty, the vision
of the Virgin as she had stooped to him so sweetly from
the sky. But, even as he did so, two new sirens sent their
long, yearning wail with an ear-splitting intensity through
his temples. He put his hand to his head and shuddered
to find how pale and weak, how terribly ineffectual, the
image of the Virgin seemed beside the message they
brought, and beside the raucous blare from all those steam-
organs, and beside the smooth incessant powerful clank of
all that machinery and beside the voices of the showmen
calling him to pleasure, calling him to pleasure.

As if to escape the coarse, obliterating impressions of
his environment, Sultan now stepped over the low railing
and with his fingers in his ears walked slowly towards the
centre of the Ash-Heap. It was useless; yet he refused to
admit that it was so even to himself, and even as, in answer
to the yearning sirens, the whole spring-tide of his
shameless Eastern blood seemed to rise within him in one
long starving wail after more happiness, more pleasure,
after the lost luxuries of the seraglio, even in that moment,
infuriated by his own uncontrollable change of temper, he
shouted at the stars three pitiful and enormous lies:

"I have found the Beloved! I desire nothing! I am at
Peace!" Half conscious of his dishonesty, he stooped
savagely as he spoke the last word, and plucking the red
rose from its little stalk, pressed it with a vindictive, almost
lustful intensity, to his lips.

He started. For at the same instant he heard, close

beside him, a low, mischievous laugh. It was a woman's laugh, but when he looked round, there was no woman, nor indeed any other creature to be seen. Sultan held the Rose at arm's length before his face and began gazing at it, as if it must have been the cause of his bewilderment. It was dark now over the Ash-Heap and the sky immediately above was powdered with stars, in spite of the glare thrown up by the myriad illuminations of the Amusement Park. Out of the column of darkness rising into the air above the Heap the little Rose seemed to glow at him more brightly than ever. And at last Sultan realised that it was not merely glowing but also singing to him. It was singing something like this:

Earth despairs not, though her Spark
    Underground is gone –
Roses whisper after dark
    Secrets of the Sun.

Sultan listened to the song which as yet he only half understood, as if entranced. When it was over, he pressed the Rose once more devoutly to his lips and as he did so, bethought him, for the first time, that it would also be possible to visit the *further* side of the Ash-Heap. He immediately climbed to the top of the Heap and began to descend the other slope.

Sultan was greatly surprised to find that the other side differed considerably from the one to which he was accustomed. Instead of consisting of a single smooth slope, it was curiously scooped out, so as to leave in one place a considerable hollow. The bottom of this hollow was nearly flat, and the side nearest the centre of the Heap rose above it in a small vertical cliff. A dilapidated old door leaned up against this side, and in the hollow, as on the rest of the great Ash-Heap, there was a good deal of debris lying about. There were some old wooden seats from a set of swings which had evidently fallen out of use, some odd straps and bits of leather, that looked as if they had to do with horses, and in the midst of all, to Sultan's great delight, one of those old-fashioned small roundabouts for children, in which the seats are wooden horses and the whole thing is worked, not by machinery, but by a man standing in the middle and turning a handle. In the Amusement Park itself this type of roundabout had long since been superseded.

Sultan began examining the debris and, in doing so, came at last to the old door. Whereupon he discovered that it was not merely leaning up against the ashen cliff as he had supposed, but actually fitted in a frame, which in its turn was built into the cliff. He tried the handle and, when he found the door locked, whipped out in an instant his little steel key. It fitted. Sultan turned the key in the lock and opened the door inwards.

VII

HE WALKED A long way without meeting anyone, down a winding dim-lit passage which at last opened into a huge, vaulted chamber, roughly circular in shape, in the centre of which stood a large Marquee. Sultan stopped and while he stood, looking wonderingly at the chamber, there emerged from one of the entrances of the Marquee a tall dignified man dressed in shirt-sleeves and riding-breeches and carrying under his arm a long whip. He walked without hurrying up to Sultan, and when he was within speaking distance, said to him, in a voice which, for some strange reason, filled him with happiness and made him look more closely at the speaker's handsome, bearded face, "Good evening! I wonder what I can do for you. I am afraid we have closed for the day!" Sultan enquired, not without an involuntary answering smile, what place it might be that he had blundered on, and then immediately began to apologise for intruding.

"Don't apologise!" interrupted the tall man a little more abruptly than before, and he explained that the Marquee contained a circus, and was one of the ordinary side-shows of the Fair, to which anybody was entitled to come. Sultan asked if it were much frequented.

"We hardly get a soul!" replied the tall man frankly. "The truth is, horses are gone quite out of fashion! Indeed," he added confidentially, "we are really engaged not so much in giving actual performance as in rehearsing for a future one." He then explained that he himself was the Ringmaster and at the same time the Proprietor of the circus.

Sultan expressed his surprise that he should have chosen this particular spot for their rehearsals, since Abdol no doubt exacted an exorbitant rent. The Ringmaster smiled.

"We pay no rent!" he said. "The money does not exist, even in fancy, which Abdol would accept from us for permission to play here. Fortunately we do not require his permission. Often enough has he tried every means, both fair and foul, to evict us but, you see, Sir, I happen to have title-deeds dating back to before the Fire."

"Then it is owing to *you*", exclaimed Sultan, his eyes opening wider, "that the great Ash-Heap has been left untouched!   I have you to thank!" The Ringmaster nodded, smiling again.

Sultan asked many more questions, and finally why, since the ground belonged to him, the Ringmaster had chosen to conceal his circus underground in this mysterious way. He explained that it was for safety.

"We have nothing to fear from Abdol, who cannot hurt us, much as he would like to. It is Abdol's customers of whom we have to beware. Therefore, in order that they should come one at a time, if they come at all, I had the outer door locked and arranged with Abdol himself that each person should be given a private key, as soon as he enters the Park. At present, alas, most of them lose their key before they have been in the Park five minutes. Consequently, we never see them!" Sultan informed the Ringmaster that Abdol had evidently abandoned this practice, and that he himself had only contrived to get in owing to his possession of a master-key. Upon this the Ringmaster grew terribly angry.

"The old Deceiver!" he cried out and began striding up and down outside the Marquee cracking his long whip, whose loud reports echoed strangely and fiercely through the vaulted chamber, while Sultan looked down in embarrassment at the Rose which he still carried in his hand.

At last the Ringmaster became calmer, and Sultan began to enquire further about the Circus and the nature of the performance for which they were rehearsing. Before long he was asking the Ringmaster if he might join the company himself. The Ringmaster showed no surprise.

"You will begin as a clown," he said in a quiet businesslike voice. "It is the way they all begin. You will learn first of all to undress at full speed, standing; and you will sign an undertaking from this day on never to remove your clothes, together with such other garments as I shall add to them, until you can do so."

Sultan was taken aback.

"B-but," he stammered, "it will be *years*! I am quite a stranger to trick-riding. I have, it is true, ridden horses bareback but that was long ago, in Asia. We sat easily. Man and horse were as one beast. Oh Sir! I shall break my neck!" For an instant the Ringmaster was as angry as before.

"And what else are necks for?" he flashed out. Sultan deliberated for a moment.

"I will sign!" he said at last. They went into the Marquee together.

Later, the Ringmaster showed him another underground chamber, in which were rows of wooden cubicles, in one of which he himself could sleep. Then he said good-night to Sultan, who thought he noticed once more an extraordinary kindness in his voice, and left him alone. The stables could not be far away. A muffled noise reached the cubicle of horses, moving about and champing in the distance, and it was to this music that, tired out as he was, Sultan quickly fell asleep in his clothes.

When he awoke the next morning, he found beside his bed a nondescript heap of old garments, which he was obliged, by his vow, to put on over those which he already wore. It was an indescribable collection. Large and small, clean and dirty, (and some of them were very dirty) male and female, somehow or other he had to get them all on to his back and his disgust positively touched fainting-point, when he was obliged to draw on, last of all, and over all the rest an absurd and rather dirty pair of pink oriental women's trousers. It seemed to him that he should certainly die of shame if anyone saw him. He was therefore greatly relieved to learn that, outside the circus tent itself, performers were allowed to wear a long black cloak, which gave them at any rate some faint resemblance to other people.

The same morning the Ringmaster took him to the stables to choose a horse. Determined to atone for the momentary weakness which had angered the master on the previous day Sultan promptly picked the largest and fieriest steed he could see, a huge black Arabian charger with a wicked eye and a magnificent stride.

This time it was the Ringmaster himself who warned him of danger.

"This kind is dangerous for the beginner!" he said. "There is too much of Abdol's strain in them! I was unable to keep it all out. Better choose another!" But Sultan insisted on his choice and observed with great pleasure that the Ringmaster himself was pleased that he did so. The latter even condescended to crack a joke with the novice, who now stood holding the black horse by the bridle and sweating under the quadruple and fantastic burden of his motley garments.

"Room for two on that horse!" said the Ringmaster, and Sultan fancied there was an especially friendly gleam in his eyes as he spoke. They both laughed.

There followed for Sultan from that day, and for many a long day afterwards, a time of hard practice. It was as rough as it was regular. Abba, the Arab steed, did not like his new master's looks and he frequently succeeded in throwing him, encumbered as he was with his extraordinary burden of heterogeneous clothing. More than once Sultan had his bones broken by these falls and on one occasion he lay at death's door, unconscious of everything that was going on around him, for many days on end. The heavy jars which each of these accidents occasioned him, and the subsequent pain of his bruises would sometimes cause him to lose all hope, even all inclination, to succeed in his undertaking and he would probably have given up and gone away, had not the pattern of fortitude, which he had once observed and admired in his friend the Philosopher, come to his aid and stood him in good stead. On the other hand, when this capacity for fortitude was itself undermined by doubts of a more intellectual nature, and a certain distrust even of the Ringmaster entered his heart, insinuating to his despondency that there was no *reason* to continue his pains — then the graceful figure and haunting melodies of the Poet, with their promise of mysterious rewards, would hover and ring in his fancy, convincing him almost against his will that what he was doing must be worth while.

After the last serious accident, Sultan began to progress more steadily and to gain a surer hope. For, curiously enough, from this time on, Abba abandoned some of his most mischievous ways, as if he were convinced at last that his rider was his master. Sultan fancied secretly that the horse had half expected he would not have the pluck to come back after that last throw, and that, when he found he was mistaken, he had given in. Gradually a deep affection sprang up between man and beast, so that they would both feel quite melancholy when night came and obliged them to part.

One night, after parting affectionately from Abba, Sultan lay on his bed, tossing restlessly in the ever increasing discomfort of his ignominious garb, itching, perspiring, and quite unable to sleep, when he felt sure he heard an impatient whinneying in the stables. "That is Abba's voice!" he cried, and the thought suddenly came to him that, being less tired than on previous nights, they might both employ a few more of the precious hours in practice. The only thing that made him hesitate was his uncertainty whether the rules of the place would allow it. He determined therefore to consult one of the more advanced performers, who had already acquired his balance and thus passed out of the clown stage — or, as they were accustomed to say in the circus vernacular — "slipped his Motley." On entering the cubicle of one of these, who was also a particular friend of his, Sultan was surprised to find it empty. He passed on to another cubicle. This, too, was unoccupied! More and more perplexed Sultan ended by trying every cubicle in the place which he knew to belong to an advanced pupil. Every single one was empty! Tired of his failures, therefore, Sultan now continued his way, without attempting to rouse any of his fellow Motleys, to the stables, where he found Abba snorting, shuffling with his feet, and pawing the ground impatiently. The horse whinneyed when he saw his master, and at once ceased shuffling. Sultan led the great black charger through the darkness of the unilluminated subterranean passages, to the vaulted chamber, which was also lampless, though a soft light glimmered through the canvas from the interior of the Marquee. He hurried towards the entrance, and was surprised to find it barred by the tall figure of the Ringmaster.

"I have come for night-practice, Sir," he said. The Ringmaster shook his head, with stern disapproval.

"But," said Sultan obstinately, his eyes on the light which glimmered through the tent, "some of the others are doing it. Why should not I?"

"*They* are not practicing," replied the Ringmaster briefly, "they are keeping the Revels!" Sultan hesitated. But the master's words only inflamed his curiosity.

"Let me just peep!" he begged in a foolish weak voice,

and, the moment he had spoken, he fancied that a change came over the Ringmaster's dark figure. Standing there with his back to the light so that Sultan could not see his face, he seemed to grow taller — to tower over the intruder with the fierce threatening gestures of an ogre.

"Back! Back!" he thundered out in a terrible voice. "Let me hear no more of it! Who sent you? *Your* time is not yet — Motley!"

Abba shivered and Sultan, too, shrank back in dismay. But before long his misery overcame his terror:

"Oh Sir!" he stammered out, "I am so tired, so tired! May I not at least take off these hideous, dripping clothes — once — just this once?" To which the Ringmaster replied in words that bit through Sultan's heart like ice:

"Yes — if you have *still* not had enough of broken vows!" Sultan slunk away abashed, leading Abba beside him, and, as he left the hollow chamber, threw one lingering look back at the soft-glimmering Marquee and at the tall figure of the Ringmaster standing dark and motionless in the doorway. Suddenly a transitory gleam lit up the master's face. Its expression was dreadful. And the arms which he had raised when he cried "Back!" and which he still held up, as if to bar the way for ever, were like two fiery serpents.

The next morning, however, the Ringmaster spoke to Sultan as if nothing at all had happened during the night. His manner was as gentle and kindly as ever, and indeed Sultan wondered how he could ever have been so much afraid of him. Later on in the day he took Sultan aside and told him that, if he really wished to continue practising by night, there was a small annexe not far from the Marquee in which he could do so. Some of the Motleys, said the Ringmaster, were already availing themselves of it. Sultan wondered why none of them had said anything to him about it.

From that time on he made use of the annexe nearly every night, though not at first for very long at a time, since he grew so quickly tired. His progress was now much more rapid, and he found himself at the same time becoming awake to much that he had formerly hardly noticed or, at best, misunderstood, in the routine and organisation of the circus. For example, there was an institution known as a Godiva-Send. Each Motley, on the day when he passed his final clown's test and threw off his clothes, became known as a "Godiva." And from time to time one of these Godivas would start out early in the morning, riding forth naked on horseback into the outside world, upon a mission whose nature Sultan still only dimly understood. Very little fuss was made over these expeditions and it was a long time before Sultan even discovered the place from which they started. He became aware much sooner of their *return* in the evening. Here the story was nearly always the same. Breathless, wounded, cruelly beaten, and covered with the excremental filth and slime which had been flung at them by crowds who had long ago become unable to bear the sight of either a horse or nakedness, they crawled back at night to the Ash-Heap and lay unconscious for many days under the tender care of the Ringmaster, who was the Physician as well as the Leader of the troupe.

All these things, as he became more fully aware of

them, began to arouse in Sultan a new curiosity about the circus and the precise object for which all this rehearsal was being conducted. He began to speak more freely about them to his companions and found that many rumours were current among them; of which, however, the most persistent was this absurd one: that it was all for fear of the electric dragons on the roundabouts in the Amusement Park!

"Why, what can there be to fear from them?" asked Sultan.

"Ah, unless they were to come alive!"

Finally Sultan summoned all his courage and actually asked the Ringmaster himself if there were any truth in this grotesque rumour. He nodded.

"What! Will the dragons really come alive, then?" And Sultan thought he detected once again a particularly friendly twinkle in the smile with which the Ringmaster looked at him, as he replied with quiet significance: –

"Everything will come alive!"

Sultan observed that, during the days immediately following a Godiva-Send, there was always a slow but steady trickle of new candidates for admission to the troupe. In this way, as time passed, their numbers swelled to an astounding degree, so that in time elaborate tunnelling operations had to be conducted, and the dimensions, both of the vaulted chamber and of the Marquee enlarged. Sultan was particularly delighted when, among the stream of new recruits, there arrived at the circus first the Philosopher and, a long time afterwards, the Poet. In the atmosphere of the circus the Poet and the Philosopher quickly gained a respect for each other which they had formerly lacked, and the three became firm friends.

The progress of the Poet was astonishing. His natural grace and dexterity stood him in good stead and his balance was so excellent that he started night-practice almost as soon as he arrived. On the other hand, he found the various restrictions which were imposed by the regulations on all members of the troupe much more irksome than either of the other two. He liked luxury, and the irritation with which he supported the incessant burden of uncomfortable and ill-fitting garments was terrible to see. Worst of all, they made him ugly and ridiculous in the eyes of his fellows! On several occasions Sultan and the Philosopher had to take him by both arms and hold him back by main force from absconding. Sultan, who felt a certain contempt on these occasions for his friend, could not escape a pang of disgust when, long before he or the Philosopher were *nearly* ready to take the test, the Poet slipped his Motley amid universal applause and joined the company of the Godivas. It was hard to understand.

As to the Philosopher, since he was thoroughly accustomed already to denying himself, he experienced none of the Poet's exquisite tortures of irritation. On the other hand his hobbledehoydom was appalling. Ride bare-back! — he could *just* about manage to sit a horse, if you first provided it with an elaborate apparatus of saddles, stirrups, blinkers, snaffles, and special leaden horseshoes to keep it from moving too fast! Moreover his congenital laziness kept him back. It was months before he would even admit that there *was* such a thing as night-practice!

Moreover, he had picked a much larger and more mettlesome steed than the Poet's.

Yet even the Philosopher slipped his Motley before poor Sultan. For not only was Abba the fieriest of all the horses, but Sultan had been given a greater quantity of clothes than any of the others. He also suffered from certain hereditary physical defects, and the result of all these disadvantages was that, though quite an early arrival, he was the very last of all to pass out!

At last, however, the day came when he, too, was to be tested for his clown's diploma. The spectators' benches were crowded with fellow performers. The arena was empty. It was Sultan's day. A noise like distant thunder without the entrance and Abba comes galloping in, swallowing up the ground in front of him, snuffing it up into his fiery nostrils and gulping it down behind in a waterfall of pawing hoofs. Under his withers, clinging to the long mane in mock desperation and at the same time waving gaily to the spectators, hangs Sultan. They gallop seven times around the great arena. On the eighth round Sultan hoists himself slowly on to the horse's back and sitting there as much at his ease as if he were at the chess-table passes six times more round the arena while a roar of Homeric laughter arises from the spectators at the sight of his absurd oriental trousers. Abba increases his speed. Sultan rises cautiously to his knees, to his feet, he stands on the rippling back of the rushing steed, his spine, straight as an arrow, sloping inward to the centre of the Marquee, he stands firm as the trunk of an oaktree, turning with the turning globe. At last, ah, at last, the clothes begin to be peeled off; first of all the ludicrous trousers; he kicks them neatly out of the entrance as he passes; then two pairs of tattered, worn-out boots, then more garments and yet more, until at last, upon great Abba going like the wind, his eyes fixed levelly before him in a trance that makes them seem to be both shut and open at the same time, he stands erect, naked from top to toe, waving his two arms above his head, and revelling in the glory of the cool air about his tortured skin.

There was a roar of applause as with a final turn and a wave of the hand, Sultan passed out through the entrance of the Marquee. Outside, the Ringmaster immediately came up to him, congratulated him warmly, made much of Abba and keeping an affectionate hand on the latter's mane, guided the pair to a part of the caves of which Sultan as yet knew nothing. Here, in a chamber hollowed out of the rocks below the Ash-Heap, roofed with crystal and pillared with stalactites, a hot mineral spring poured its waters with an incessant gurgling music into a natural cup or basin, which art had lipped with marble and alabaster. The Ringmaster looked significantly at Sultan.

"Take your time!" he said, "Bathe yourself and your horse at leisure. You have no further duties until to-night, when it will be your privilege, as complete Godiva, to join the Revels! And to-morrow — the dress rehearsal of your second turn!" He smiled gravely at both of them and then turned and left the cave.

Night came. Timidly, now that the hour had come, timidly and shyly, Sultan approached the great glimmering Marquee. The very nakedness, for which he had so longed, seemed to abash him, now that he had achieved it, until, at the entrance, the Ringmaster welcomed him in the friendliest manner and spoke words which made him feel at home. Sultan passed into the Marquee. It was difficult to believe that it was the same place, as that in which he had so often practised and at last triumphed. The light, by its very softness, was dim, so that, to begin with, he could not see far. He observed, however, that the dry sand of the arena had been converted, by some magic, into a soft green lawn of the closest and most ancient turf. Paths led here and there to the centre, where a fountain played into a crystal basin. The surrounding tiers of wooden seats, shrouded as they were in comparative darkness, might have been an enchanted forest wherein the great arena was no more than a moonlit glade, while, scattered about the turf in an unpremeditated yet delightful confusion lay all manner of mossy couches and divans. Sultan stood entranced. As far as he could see, all the men and women whom he knew during the day as members of the circus, were there, only in a slightly different form. Naked, like himself, they wandered to and fro in couples, played on the sward to the sound of music, or reposed on the divans sometimes singly, sometimes locked in one another's arms. What surprised him most of all was to see that many of those whom he knew in the daytime as elderly persons were here quite young, while some, whom he knew as young, were old and wise. Moreover the Revellers had not in every case retained their daytime sex. He saw friends mingling together as lovers, and lovers meeting and conversing as friends.

Sultan smiled to himself as he observed the Poet, a beautiful youth reclining perfectly at his ease, as if upon a couch, amid a galaxy of beautiful girls, with whom he was exchanging verses and caresses. He wondered how he himself should ever have the courage to break into one of these charmed circles, and for a long time he stood, hesitating and shy, beside the entrance of the Marquee. After a while, however, he observed, not far away from him, a figure with its back turned, standing alone. It was that of the Philosopher. Sultan had of late been thrown much together with his old friend, for whom he had come to feel a new and even deeper affection, since the latter had begun to remind him so strangely of his own father, long since dead. The Philosopher, who had not long been a Godiva, appeared, now, like Sultan himself, to be feeling shy and uncertain, and Sultan noticed that, unlike most of the others, he still looked quite elderly standing there with his shoulders bent and his head a little sunken, as he had so often stood when he came in after a hard morning in the arena. It almost looked as if, in his case, the mysterious process of rejuvenation had not yet had time to work in him, and, seeing him thus, Sultan's heart was suddenly shaken with compassion and his eyes drenched with tears. He thought how pleasant it would be to be able to comfort the old man's weariness and restore to him his lost youth. And, behold, at the same instant a tremor passed through his limbs and he felt the light touch of silken hair about his shoulders. Looking quickly down at himself, what was his astonishment to see that the mere thought had transformed him into a mischievous fiery-eyed little brunette! He laughed merrily, and, stealing up on tiptoe behind the old man suddenly clapped his hands over his eyes …

The next morning, Sultan stood alone in the arena.

"This is to be an original turn!" the Ringmaster said to him, "you yourself will have to decide what to do!" He stood therefore alone in the arena (for even his horse had been taken away from him), waiting, and wondering if he ought to make some move, or if he should wait for circumstances to tell him what to do. Suddenly he heard the familiar thunder of hoofs — Abba's hoofs, and in a moment the dear black horse tore in through the entrance and round and round the ring. But the marvellous thing was that on his great, broad, rippling back, perfectly poised and at her ease, her long hair streaming backward, as if frozen on the wings of the wind, stood — who but the Holy One herself, the White-skinned Dancer, the Darling, the Beloved?

"Lady!" shouted Sultan exultantly in a voice louder than the thunder of the horse's hoofs and, without a moment's hesitation, summoning to his aid all the dexterity won from his painful years of practice, he leaped up beside her and hissing to Abba the single speed-word which turned his already formidable gallop into a streak of lightning, he clasped her in his arms and covered her with kisses.

After this his whole grasp of the passage of time became confused. Sometimes it seemed to him that life in the great circus was going on very much as before, and that he spent his days practising in the arena and only occasionally saw Lady, at night, for instance, when they both attended the Revels. But at other times it seemed as though these same Revels were going on all the time, day and night, and that Lady was perpetually clasped in his arms, and that Abba never ceased his galloping or needed rest. Sometimes he awoke with a start to find he had been dreaming with extraordinary vividness that he had completed after all his intended journey back to the East, where he had long ago become a hermit, a man given up wholly to ecstatic visions, and Sultan even became so confused that once or twice he fancied he had never left the seraglio.

Once — or was it many times, hundreds of times? — a loud cry of

"The dragons! The dragons!"

rang through the Marquee like an alarum, whereupon Abba rushed of his own accord out of the arena, along the passage, and into the daylight. In the hollow outside they found the little wooden horses on the derelict children's roundabout on the point of turning into baby unicorns, but Sultan seized the brass rod from the back of one of them which was not yet transformed, and it immediately turned into a lance which the two of them, Lady and himself, clasped and wielded as a single warrior. They rode forthwith over the Ash-Heap out into the Amusement Park, where they found a scene of hideous confusion. The great electric dragons were one by one coming to life and proceeding promptly to devour first the human beings who had been riding on their backs and then others. Men, women and children disappeared into the crunching, crackling jaws grinning in the most horrible convulsions of agony, while Sultan and Lady rode to and fro, selecting, wherever they could, a dragon which had not yet devoured its man and plunging, as Abba reared indignantly over the hideous monster with twitching and dilated nostrils, their lance into its gaping jaws. Behind them the half-slain dragons lay writhing on the ground, occasionally twitching in violent spasms as they spat out a crackling length of blue spark, until the little unicorns, running to and fro, finished them off with a single sharp butt of their irresistible horns.

Sultan and Lady returned to the Marquee, which immediately began to rock to and fro upon the bosom of an approaching earthquake. The ground heaved. Buildings began to fall. Fires broke out. With one terrific shock the sides of the great Ash-Heap fell apart and the Marquee rose bodily to the surface of the earth. In the midst of the Arena the tall Ringmaster stood, cracking his long whip and calling to all the company to maintain their presence of mind, and, above all, to keep their balance. Round and round the ring thundered the horses to the rhythmical crack of his whip, until slowly a curious new sound began to attract the attention of all: –

Pt!   Pt!   Pt!   Pt!

on the roof and sides of the Marquee. Somebody went outside to investigate and, rushing in again, reported that the automatic cigarette machines had come alive and were firing off their contents at the Marquee like machine-guns. Some of them struck the canvas with such force that they penetrated to the interior, whereupon they immediately changed back into the living tobacco-plant, the paper turning into white butterflies and fluttering away while the golden colour of the weed remained hovering about the blossom in a little aureole of fragrance.

More and more of the appurtenances of the Amusement Park came to life. As soon as the automatic machines had exhausted their stock of cigarettes, they rushed madly off and began copulating with the automatic tarts and the pornographic photographs in the stereoscopes. Once again the whole circus-troupe dashed forth and did all it could to save the miserable survivors from the appalling offspring of these obscene unions, which were growing and multiplying like gigantic lice in the warmth from the numerous conflagrations. Here all save the troupe themselves were helpless, for without horses to keep a man above the level of the omnivorous vermin, there was no hope of survival. And now, owing to the astonishing speed, power, and dexterity of Abba, none was able to do such effective rescue-work as Sultan himself. More and more of the appurtenances of the Amusement Park came alive, and even the generating stations, dotted here and there about the Park, turned into a species of colossal spider, drawing fat, black power-cables up under them like living, hairy legs while the systems of light-cables turned into complicated nets in which human-beings became entangled, hanging paralysed and seeming dead, though actually conscious in every screaming nerve, until some great dynamo crawled out along its copper excrement and electrocuted them with a still stronger current.

At the end of the last nightmare, the whole troupe returned to the Marquee, where the Ringmaster commanded them sternly, whatever they heard or saw, not to leave the arena again. He had work for them now within. And, even as he spoke, a spark from one of the fires fell on the roof of the Marquee, which burst into flames, shrivelled together and soared up into the sky, while the canvas sides fell apart like the petals of a flower. The arena began to widen itself like a ripple on a stone-plashed pool. Faster and faster round it flew the horses and in the centre stood the Ringmaster, cracking his whip and shouting exhortation to the troupe. Lady suddenly pointed up to the sky. Sultan's eyes, following her finger, rested on the crescent Moon:

"It's nearer!"

he shouted to her, astonished, above the din, and she nodded and smiled, as if nothing unexpected were happening. From beyond the circle of the arena came now the sound of catastrophe after catastrophe, with a noise as of falling cities. The whole air was full of lamentation, full of voices calling:

"Ah Woe! ... Ah Woe! ... Ah Woe! ..."

in slow lugubrious tones, which rose and went moaning on with a dreary insistence, so that at last there seemed to be nothing anywhere in the world but only this Ah Woe! ... Ah Woe! ... Ah Woe! ... of which it was made — the great full-mouthed "Ah"s and the mournful rounded "O"s, until the very galloping of the horses fell into the rhythm of their alternation and the steady beat of the sighing piteous "Ah" was taken up inside the Arena by the troupe itself, resounding from their circle of sleeping-waking mouths and going up into the sky in a great enchanted yawn.

Gradually Sultan became aware that a fresh sound was insinuating itself, a mysterious hiss which seemed to arise out of the original sounds, and to mingle with them rhythmically, and yet also to oppose them. Where did it come from? From the Ringmaster, who was calling out slowly, regularly, again and again and again,

"Kiss! ... Kiss! ... Kiss! ..."

but with such rhythmic pauses, that his voice always followed a renewed burst of wailing, so that, as the sullen ocean breaking on a long low shore moans and then sharply hisses while the waters are dragged reluctantly back over the resisting shingle, so these two opposite sounds, continually following one another, mingled together in Sultan's ears! Ah Woe! ... Kiss! ... Ah Woe! ... Kiss! Ah Woe! ... Kiss! ... rising and falling, rising and falling, as if they had been going on for ever. He looked at Lady significantly, too eager to obey what seemed to be a peremptory command of the Ringmaster, addressed indifferently to all the couples on the circling steeds. But for a moment she turned her face away — and with a mocking laugh pointed again at the Moon, which hung over the arena, by now an enormous size and still approaching rapidly. Her face seemed to suggest that she thought the Ringmaster had been addressing, not the Earth, but the Moon. Sultan looked again. The Ringmaster stood like a tall captain upon the prow of a vessel, to which another vessel is approaching, calling calmly and sternly the orders which will bring them safely alongside. The Moon rushed down nearer. And now for the first time Sultan could perceive how the darker half of it is composed, not as he had always imagined, of rock and black shadow but all of interweaving furious flames — clear blood-reds and brilliant Mediterranean-blues — leaping in a pursed silence, uncontrollably out of themselves, like the secret transports of a soul too enraptured to speak. He turned his eyes to her and, as he did so, the ground opened under their feet. Answering flames shot up from beneath them. Lady returned his ardent gaze. They burst together into floods of tears and fell to kissing one another, and, in an instant, erect on Abba's rippling back they had melted into one, their four lower limbs struggling downwards like intertwining roots while their two touching breasts strained together and upward in an endless ecstasy of desire that was at the same time fruition. The hoofs of the horses thundered on the flames. In the centre of the ever-widening Arena stood the Ringmaster, grown now to gigantic stature, his arms outstretched above his head and forming a great cup. Suddenly all took fire, melted into one, became a chalice of living flames, the petals of a giant Sun-flower into which the journeying Moon fell with a long sigh of relief.

The bookplate of Owen Barfield from c. 1953
by Josephine Grant Watson

Lightning Source UK Ltd.
Milton Keynes UK
22 September 2009

144010UK00001B/37/P

9 780955 958229